THE NESTS ARE EMPTY

Mary Kay

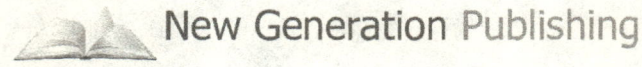 New Generation Publishing

CHAPTER ONE

Donny Harris looked once more at the walls of the old mine tunnel and nodded. That's it Chris we've finished here, he told his assistant. They packed their equipment away and moved off towards the cage lift that would carry them to the surface. The sun was shining and as Donny breathed the fresh air, he wondered briefly why he had chosen to be a Mining Engineer as his profession, but he had always been fascinated by holes in the ground ever since he had fallen down an old mine Air- Shaft, when he was a child.

He had been offered a prestigious position at Head Office, perhaps he should consider the offer and become more settled, it's something I might seriously consider now I'm older. I'll talk it over with Dad, he decided.

Back at the hotel, Chris disappeared into his room with a wave of his hand. Donny ordered a room service meal and went to shower.

As Donny left the shower a towel wrapped around his waist his Mobile phone rang, Hi Mum how are you? He asked. I'm fine, but when are you coming home? She replied. A couple more days and I should be back for good. Donny said. What do you mean? His Mother asked. I've been offered an executive job at Head Office and have almost decided to take it. I want to discuss it with Dad first, but I feel that I've done enough jetting all over the world and its time to settle down. He replied. Oh that's wonderful news darling does that mean you will be bringing that lovely girl Bettina with you? Janet asked. No Mum, that lovely girl has gone off with a lovely 'Rich' boy. Donny said ruthfully. Oh I'm so sorry darling. Janet sympathised. Don't be sorry Mum, it didn't hurt my heart only my pride, no doubt there'll be another one come by some time, girls like her are ten- a- penny. Donny replied. I must go Mum I'm still wet from the shower.

A knock on the door heralded the arrival of a waitress

with his ordered meal. The young girl gasped with embarrassment and would have backed out of the room but Donny said jokingly, Hey don't take my supper away I'm starving. I'm so s-s-sorry stuttered the girl, and putting the tray down on to the table she hurried away.

The next morning Donny went down to breakfast hoping to see the pretty little waitress again, he wanted to apologise for embarrassing her. Belinda Jones was due to serve breakfast and hoped that the attractive man in room 40 would not appear. But to her consternation there he was at one of her tables. She put on a blank expression and went to take his order, thinking 'Please don't let him recognise me, 'but no such luck, Donny had been waiting for her. She took his order for breakfast but kept her eyes down and would have been annoyed if she had seen the amused expression on Donny's face, for he guessed that she was hoping he would not recognise her. How could he not remember such a pretty, graceful, blue- eyed, natural blonde? He looked at her nametag 'Belinda Jones' Belinda suits you; it's a pretty name. He remarked. But she walked away quickly to fetch his order from the kitchen. When his breakfast was placed on the table Donny looked up from his newspaper and asked her. Would you have dinner with me tonight Belinda? I'm on duty Sir. Belinda politely refused. We're not allowed to fraternise with the guests she added. I'm checking out later so I won't be a guest. Donny replied. Belinda looked at the handsome face with its piercing blue eyes and the thick chestnut hair and she almost weakened but instead she said. Are you trying to get me dismissed Sir? No, Donny replied. I'm trying to make a date with you. The name's Donny Harris. He said holding out a hand prepared to shake hers. Belinda looked at him in amazement and shook her head. Am I that repulsive? He asked. No, but you are dangerous. Belinda replied. Men like you eat girls like me for breakfast, so thanks but no thanks Mr Harris. And turning away she crossed the room and disappeared through the door marked 'Staff Only'. Donny gazed after her thoughtfully.

Well, he thought, Miss Belinda Jones you certainly know how to put a fellow in his place.

When Belinda came off duty that afternoon she found Donny waiting outside in the staff car park, he was leaning casually against the bonnet of an expensive saloon car. He was dressed in expensive casual clothes and Belinda's pulse gave a jolt. Wow he was really a 'Dream Boat' she thought, but pretending not to notice him she walked past. Am I invisible as well as dangerous now? Donny asked to her retreating back. Belinda was tempted to keep walking, but good manners prevailed and she turned round. You're very persistent Mr Harris. She said. Yes, It's my middle name. Donny replied. Please come out for a while, we could go to tea somewhere and you can be waited on for a change. Belinda hesitated but Donny looked so nice and somehow for some reason she felt that she could trust him. They went to a quiet little 'tea'shop' with pots of tea and homemade scones and cakes. Donny tucked in heartily and Belinda wondered how he kept his athletic figure. 'Belinda Jones,' that sounds very Welsh, do you come from Wales? Donny asked, after Belinda had poured the tea. No, but my father was Welsh and when he was killed in a mine disaster my mother packed up and went to London to live and care for her maiden aunt. I was a baby and between them I suppose I must have been spoiled. It doesn't show. Donny said smiling. Is this your real job, in Hotels I mean? He asked.. Oh no it's a holiday job; I'm at the music college in London, taking piano and singing she replied. Really? That's a coincidence. One of my cousins is there, her name is Beth Parry do you know her? Donny asked. Oh yes Belinda replied, she's very talented. She has a beautiful singing voice, she is taking piano and Violin and she's brilliant, I think she's hoping to go into one of the big Orchestras. What about you? Donny asked. I'm hoping to teach in schools, not ordinary schools, but schools for children with disabilities both mental and physical, Music is such a healer you know. She replied.

You should talk to my Aunt Anna; she 's a strong

believer in all that Holistic and Meditation stuff.

Although I must say that it did work on me. When I was a kid, I fell down a disused mine shaft vent and had Panic attacks and nightmare afterwards, but my aunt's friend helped me. Belinda was horrified.

How old were you? She asked, I was five years Old. Donny replied. When I was growing up, I was always getting myself into a fix, I even managed to get myself kidnapped, and another time, I narrowly missed burning down the house by attempting to light a Campfire, in my Bedroom. If it hadn't been for our Nanny who rescued us all, I wouldn't be here now. Oh your poor mother she must have been distraught. Belinda Exclaimed. Yes I guess she was. Donny replied. And she wasn't too happy when I chose to be a Mining Engineer, but she didn't try to stop me, although she would have preferred that I went into law and became a Barrister, the same as my Dad and Uncle Drew. But my brother Jamie and cousin Jonathan have followed in their two father's footsteps so that lets me off the hook. I used to go to their Chambers when I was a Teenager to help as a holiday job and I always thought how dull it was. It sounds as if you have a very big family. Belinda said, feeling envious. There's only me now since Aunty and Mum have passed away.

I'm sorry for your loss, Donny said sympathetically. I have two sisters as well. Annabel and Caitlin they are photographic models. They're twins, but actually part of triplets with Jamie as the third baby. Good heavens your mother must be a 'saint' to cope with all of you Belinda exclaimed.

Yes she is pretty 'special', she never complained about my wandering all over the world, even though she must have been worried sick about the dangers of my job. But my travels have made me realise that there's no place like England. I could never settle anywhere else. Well that's enough of the personal histories, what would you like to do, and how long have you got before you go back on duty? Donny asked.

They went to a local Museum which Donny had found interesting because it mentioned the old mine where he had been working that week. Soon Belinda had to be back and prepare to go on duty for the evening meals. They parted company reluctantly on both their parts. Donny decided to stay on at another hotel so that he could continue to see Belinda. He suspected that he was becoming seriously attracted to her and he hoped that she was feeling the same.

Donny couldn't wait to see Belinda again, and next morning after breakfast he went to the Hotel where Belinda was working. Enquiring for her at Reception brought unwelcome news, Belinda had gone back to London her job was done and the College term would soon begin. At first Donny was puzzled. What had he done to make Belinda go without saying Goodbye? Then he remembered her reply to his first asking her for a date. You're dangerous Mr Harris; men like you eat girls like me for breakfast. Was he such an ogre? I suppose I was rather high handed in getting her to go out with me, I guess I deserve the snub. I've been out with so many 'Good Time Girls' that I've forgotten how to treat a really nice girl. Beth has warned me so many times that I'll meet my match one day and it looks as if she was right, he thought gloomily.

As he walked engrossed in his gloomy thoughts, he suddenly noticed that a grubby little dog was following him. Hullo boy, where did you spring from? He bent to pat its head and noticed that it wore no collar. Aha! A 'run away' are you? The little dog rolled onto its back, inviting him to scratch its stomach. Donny obliged, and suddenly realised how thin and bony it was. You need a good meal old chap, are you lost? The dog wagged its tail. Donny rose and began to walk on, but the little dog followed him and would not be deterred. Spying a police station opposite he picked the dog up and crossed the road. The desk sergeant was sympathetic but had no record of a lost dog matching this ones description. I can put him in the dog pound Sir. The sergeant offered. What will happen to him then? Asked Donny. Well he'll stay for a few days and then we'll pass him on. Donny didn't ask where too, he had a good idea what the dog's fate would be, and he didn't like to think of it. I'll keep him, but thanks for your trouble he replied and taking the dog he left. Outside the station he stopped to consider. Finally he made a decision he would keep the dog himself. Well Buddy, it looks as if you and I are going to stick together, but first you need a wash and brush up and a meal. The dog looked up at him with such appealing eyes it touched his heart and he made up his mind that no matter what he would keep him. He took the little dog to a Dog Parlour for a thorough wash, complete with flea powder and worming tablets. The owner was very knowledgeable and gave him some useful tips, and finally having purchased two feeding bowls, dog food, a collar and lead and a dog basket it was time to head for home.

On arrival in London he first phoned his mother to tell her that he was 'safely' home, and of his rescued pet, and then he went to call on Beth. When he arrived he could hear the piano. Beth was playing a Chopin Waltz and the beautiful notes held him silent until she had finished, then he knocked on the door. Beth was pleased and surprised to see him, she offered to make coffee and he followed her into the kitchen. Who's this? She asked when she saw Buddy. We adopted each other up in Birmingham Donny said, and explained how he had come to own Buddy.

Mum's out. She said, switching on the coffee machine. Actually it was you I wanted to see, do you know a girl at college called Belinda Jones? Donny asked. Yes, she's a really lovely girl what do you want with her? I'm warning you Donny don't try treating her as you do most of the girls you date, she's a lovely sensitive girl and I won't let you hurt her. Beth said sharply. I don't want to hurt her, replied Donny, quite the opposite in fact, we met yesterday at the Hotel where I was staying, she was working there and I'm afraid that I bounced her into going out with me for the afternoon. We only went for tea and then to the local Museum. I've never felt so happy with anyone, you're right she is a sweet girl and I really want to see her again. Donny replied. Beth looked thoughtful. I don't know where she lives, but when I go into class tomorrow I'll ask her if she wants to see you again, that's the best I can do I'm afraid, Beth said. You're a 'Star' thanks so much. Donny said hugging her. I promise my motives are honourable. Just don't make me sorry I promised to help you that 's all. Beth replied sternly.

Donny couldn't concentrate on the report that he was writing and in the end he gave up and went to visit his mother. Taking Buddy with him. Janet was delighted to see him and wasn't surprised at the appearance of Buddy, she was used to Donny's impulsive actions and she made a fuss of Buddy giving him a biscuit. She wanted to hear how his work had gone, and was he sure that he wanted an office job, after his previous exciting job. Donny assured her that he'd had his fill of excitement and was now ready to settle for a quieter life. They discussed it for a while, and then Donny told his mother about Belinda. Janet listened quietly while Donny was talking and she sensed that this girl was going to be different from any other girl that he had dated. But it seemed his reputation had gone before him and Belinda was wisely cautious.

After two days Donny couldn't wait any longer and phoned Beth to ask what Belinda had said. Beth told him that she had given his message and his phone number to Belinda and that was all she could do to help him, and 'No' she was not going to ask Belinda for her address, for obvious reasons.

CHAPTER TWO

The report was finished at last and Donny pressed the 'Send' button. Lifting his arms above his head he stretched, relieving his aching shoulders. The sun was shining invitingly. I'll take Buddy and walk across the Park to visit Granny and Gramps, he decided .As he turned in at the Park Gates he passed an elderly lady who was walking a Poodle on a pink lead, a pink bow tied on its head. He smiled as he passed, and looking ahead, in the distance he noticed a girl walking a small pug dog. She bent and released it, immediately the little dog raced towards him; the girl began calling and running after it. Donny wondered why she was getting agitated. Then he realised that the dog was not running away, but was running towards the poodle. When the little Pug came within range of him Donny did a 'flying rugby tackle' and caught him, the Pug promptly bit him and the elderly lady with the Poodle screamed in alarm. That nasty dog was going to savage my Snowdrop she accused. No Madam. Donny replied. He was not going to 'Savage' her but more likely 'Ravish' her. Have you no more sense than to bring a female dog on heat to a public park. I advise you to take 'Snowdrop' home and keep her there for a few days. The old lady gave an offended gasp and hurried away. Donny picked up the little dog saying. Now young Pug, take my advice, if you want to get a girlfriend you have to 'Woo' her and be 'Nice' not attack her.

Is that what you do? A voice behind him asked. Turning he was surprised and delighted to see that it was Belinda. How amazing is this? Donny exclaimed. Where did you spring from? I'm the one who foolishly let Pug off his lead, Belinda replied. Oh there's blood on your hand, she said, did Pug bite you? Yes Donny replied with a grin, I rather think that he objected to my curtailing his 'Sport' with 'Lady Snowdrop' the Poodle. You must let me clean and dress your hand. Belinda insisted. Have you had a

Tetanus injection lately? Yes nurse. Donny replied solemnly his eyes twinkling. I didn't know you cared. He joked. Of course I care, I don't want you suing old Mrs Day because her dog has bitten you. Belinda said indignantly. You're still very good at putting me in my place I notice. Donny replied with mock sadness. What are you doing here anyway? He asked. I live here on the other side of the park she replied. What a coincidence, my Grandparents live there, in one of the houses facing the park. Donny said. Oh I'm nowhere so grand, I live in one of the Mews Cottages, my mother and aunty bought it together when we first came here from Wales, it's mine now that they are gone. Belinda explained. If you won't go to A and E then I insist that you let me wash and dress it, you don't want it to turn septic. I'm afraid I can't leave Buddy is it OK if he comes too.? Donny asked. Oh I hadn't noticed him in all the fuss. What a sweetie. She stooped to pat Buddy who rolled over in his usual supine position. He's adorable, but he's very thin, she said patting him. When Pug came to sniff at the new comer, he seemed to pass muster for he wagged his tail, and he watched with interest. Donny explained how he had come to have the little dog and Belinda agreed that she too would not have left him at the dog pound, for who knows what could have happened to him.

Well Pug. Donny said addressing the now passive little dog, it seems that the 'Lady' has decided to 'Patch me up' so lead the way.

Arriving at the cottage Belinda asked him. Would you wait a moment while I take Pug back to Mrs Day? Her arthritis is bad today that's why I was walking Pug, but I'm afraid I didn't do a very good job. Donny silently blessed the errant Pug for he would not have met Belinda again if she had not been walking in the park with the dog.

Presently, entering the cottage behind Belinda. Buddy settled himself down on the hearthrug and Donny looked around with interest, the front door led into a cosy sitting room with a kitchen beyond. In the corner a staircase rose up to the rooms above, Donny followed Belinda into the kitchen where she had already switched on the kettle. And had set a bowl of water down for Buddy. Would you like Tea or Coffee? She asked. Whatever you're having Donny replied. Suddenly he felt almost shy an unusual sensation for him. It must be her Mum and Aunty keeping an eye on her, he thought wryly as he seated himself in one of the comfortable armchairs. 'I couldn't live here' he thought and then wondered what had made him think that.

Belinda came in with two mugs of tea. I hope you don't mind tea, she said. But I'm trying to cut back on coffee; it's so easy to drink too much isn't it? Donny agreed that it was, and they sat in silence for a moment, then they both began to speak at once.

Donny stopped, saying, Sorry, you first, what were you going to say? I was going to ask if you're hand was painful, is it throbbing? Belinda asked. It was hurting, but Donny was not going to admit it, instead he replied. Oh I'll live don't worry about it. But Belinda rose and went into the kitchen returning with a First Aid Box, this she set on the coffee table and began to sort through it's contents. As she bent her head to look in the box her hair fell forward, and Donny longed to touch the long golden silky strands. At that moment Belinda, extracting a bottle of Iodine took the temporary bandage from his hand and swabbed the wound generously with Iodine. Donny drew in his breath with a hiss. I'm sorry Belinda apologised, but it's important to get the wound thoroughly clean .She then pasted it with anti-biotic cream and bandaged it neatly. Where did you learn to do that? Donny asked amazed at her proficiency I learned in Africa, one summer when I first went to college. Some of us went out there with a team to help in a mobile hospital, we went where they don't have access to medical help and we had to learn quite a lot of skills that we wouldn't necessarily need at home. Belinda replied..

Did you want to be a nurse? Donny asked with interest. No, not really, I just wanted to help and try to make a

10

difference, but I'm afraid I was more of a liability than help. I caught Malaria and had to be nursed before I was well enough to go home. Belinda replied with a wry smile. At least you tried to do something helpful. Donny replied, it's more than I ever did. I'm ashamed to say that as a student all I wanted to do was have a good time and enjoy myself.

Well we're all different aren't we? Belinda replied, rising and collecting the mugs. Would you like another mug of tea? She offered. No thank you. Donny replied. I must go I'm afraid, I promised to visit my Grandparents and they'll be expecting me. He still had that strange feeling as if something was urging him to stay, but he dismissed it and said his 'Goodbye's' and 'Thank you's' for her hospitality.

Alfred and Rosamond, Donny's Grandparents, were delighted to see him, for although he wasn't a blood relation they where very fond of him. When Alfred's son Seb had married Donny's mother, Janet, he had adopted Donny as a small child, and nobody ever thought of him as other than a true member of the family. .

Donny and Buddy stayed for lunch, Rosamond was very taken with Buddy and made a great fuss of him. They caught up on all the family news, but Donny didn't mention Belinda although his grandfather teased him about his numerous 'Young Ladies'.

As he and Buddy left his grandparents house, without thinking he turned in the direction of Belinda's cottage. When he realised that he was moving in the wrong direction he stopped, then for some reason he continued on towards the Mews Cottages. At Belinda's cottage he stopped and went to the door, as he raised his hand to knock the door swung open. Donny hesitated, then cautiously entered the room and received a huge shock, for the whole room was in chaos, everything turned over, chairs ripped, their stuffing spilled out onto the carpet, stunned for a moment Donny could not collect his thoughts, then he rushed towards the stairs calling out,

Belinda are you alright? Upstairs was in the same disarray as the sitting room. Frantically Donny searched the second bedroom and bathroom, but there was no sign of Belinda, and taking out his mobile he rang the police.

Where could she be? Donny stood for a moment thinking, he had searched the cottage but what about outside? As he went out of the back door he noticed that it had not been locked, warning bells rang in his head, searching the surrounding area he found that the garden shed was locked and he could see nothing through the small window When the police arrived all was bustle and questions, they were suspicious of Donny at first but his grandparents confirmed that he had been with them, and the smashed clock in the kitchen told the time when it had all happened. When Donny saw that he shivered, because it had been just after he had left, he wished now that he had listened to his premoniion instead of dismissing the feeling.

The police had searched and taken away samples, looking for clues, the cottage was cordoned off with striped tape and unofficial entry barred.

The next day, Donny felt drawn back to the site for he was sure that the clue to Belinda's disappearance was there, he walked along the ally way at the rear of the Cottages. Suddenly Buddy began to bark. What is it boy? Donny asked crouching down to him, have you smelled a rat? Buddy barked and scratched at the gate to Belinda's garden. Donny rose and looked at the end of the little garden, he paused for a moment. Buddy's barking became more urgent and Donny opening the gate entered the garden and Buddy ran at once to the shed, and his barking became even more insistent. Donny inspected the door of the shed. It was fastened with a strong lock, which the police had not opened. He found an old garden tool and began to prise the lock from the wooden door. It was dark inside the shed and smelled of damp earth, empty pots stood in rows and some sacks of Potting Mould stood beside them. Buddy was sniffing in the corner of the shed and then he barked. What is it boy have you found a mouse? Asked Donny coming to look. As his eyes became accustomed to the dim light he noticed a heap of sacks. Buddy was pulling at the heavy sacks and Donny went to help him. A shock ran through him like an electric bolt, for a face was under those sacks, it was badly battered and bruised but he recognised the beautiful blonde hair in spite of the dirt, it was Belinda.

Donny's heat missed a beat 'Please God, don't let her be dead' he prayed and almost afraid to touch her he knelt beside the prostrate little figure and felt for a pulse, it was there, but so faint it was only a quiver. 'Than you, Thank you God' said Donny the tears running down his face and jumping up he rushed to the cottage, the constable on duty was about to challenge him but when he saw Donny's face he said sharply What is it sir? In the shed, Its Belinda, Donny gasped.

An Ambulance and more police arrived. Donny insisted on going in the Ambulance with Belinda, when they told him "No" he said that he was Belinda's Fiancée and they let him go with her. One of the policemen kindly offered to take Buddy to Rosamond and explain what had happened. Belinda's condition was serious for as well as her injuries she had lain unconscious all night in a cold damp shed. Donny waited anxiously until at last a nurse came to tell him that he could go in and see Miss Jones.

Belinda lay motionless barely breathing, tubes and drips attached to her, but she's alive thought Donny gratefully. He would be having some words with whoever was in charge of this case, wasn't the shed one of the first places they should have looked in spite of the padlock, if Buddy had not made a fuss at the end of the garden and he himself had not disobeyed police orders and gone to look for her, she could have lain there and died. Donny shivered at the thought and felt a surge of anger.

Donny's grandparents, Alfred and Rosamond, had come to the hospital to support him for they could tell that he was extremely distressed and that his feelings for

Belinda were more than friendship. For Rosalind it brought back memories of the death of her own beloved daughter who had been about the same age as Belinda when she died. Gwendolyn had suffered terrible disabilities from birth, for unknown to Rosamond, her husband, when young and foolish, had caught a disease that had remained in his blood, and it had been passed on to the baby. He had blamed Rosalind for the baby's disabilities and claimed that the child was not his.

When he died she discovered that he had made a cruel Will, He had arranged that if Rosalind ever re-married she and Gwendolyn would have nothing, for although he was a very rich man he was miserly and begrudged anyone else spending his money.

Donny spent many hours sitting by Belinda's bed, talking to her and sroking her hair, anything to let her know that he was there and that he loved her. He did love her he realised that now, it was no longer the teasing game that he had light heartedly begun, he was now deeply in love and if he lost her did not know how he could bear it.

One evening as Donny sat in his usual place beside her bed Belinda gave a sigh and a groan, Donny immediately rang the buzzer beside the bed and a nurse came at once expecting the worst, but instead she found a beaming Donny. She made a Sigh and a Groan. He said excitedly. The nurse felt Belinda's pulse. I'll get the doctor she exclaimed hurrying away.

From that moment on Belinda's progress was rapid and soon she was sitting up and wanting to wash her hair and have a shower instead of a 'bed bath'

The only worry seemed to be that her memory was gone, so that when questioned by the police she could tell them nothing.

Alfred being a Barrister had once had dealings with a Detective Inspector Stanley Brent, who although retired still took a great interest in police work. Alfred happened to meet Stanley at their Club one evening and Alfred discussed the matter with him. Stanley listened with interest. Sounds to me like the return of an old 'lag 'that had hidden something valuable and wants to retrieve it. Stanley said reflectively. But what can that have to do with a young girl like Belinda? Alfred asked. If this man has been in Prison for a number of years, Belinda would have been a baby when he committed the crime. What about her father? Stanley asked. He was killed in a mine disaster years ago. Alfred replied. Mmm, How convenient, Stanley murmured thoughtfully. What part of Wales did they come from? He asked. Do you think it may have a bearing on the case? Alfred said. It's certainly one angle worth looking into. Stanley replied. Leave it with me I'll put out some feelers.

CHAPTER THREE

Belinda was now ready to be discharged from hospital, but her house was still a wreak because the police had only just finished with their search for clues and the Insurance Company had not yet settled her claim. She had nowhere to go. Rosamond and Alfred urged her to come and stay with them, Donny would have dearly loved to offer a home, but he knew that she would not have accepted. And so, much to Rosamond's delight, Belinda went to stay with Alfred and Rosamond. Buddy too seemed to have been adopted by Rosamond, for while Donny had been at the hospital with Belinda. Buddy had stayed with Rosamond and had been well cared for; he had gained weight and was now back to normal. Rosamond suggested he stay with them as Donny being at work all day, meant that Buddy would be alone. Donny was reluctant to part with him, but knew that it was the best solution.

Donny was even more in love with Belinda; she had been such a brave little soul all the way through this terrible time. He had not told Belinda of his telling the Hospital that she was his fiancée for he felt that she would not approve of his deceit even though he had been desperate. He now went back to work, for while Belinda had been ill he could not settle to anything serious. He wanted to tell her how much he loved her and wanted to marry her but he didn't think that she would believe him after the casual teasing way he had behaved when they first met.

Belinda was grateful for Alfred and Rosamond's hospitality she had been worried as to where she would live until her house was once more habitable. She had offered to pay rent but they would not hear of it and treated her as they would a Granddaughter, for secretly they hoped that she would marry Donny.

Now that Belinda was so much better she began to try and exercise her memory but became frustrated when she failed to remember anything at all. She had met all the family over the weeks and loved them all; while they thought her enchanting and secretly hoped that she would become a member of the family. Belinda found that she could still play the piano and sing, but her college work was a mystery to her, the college Principal was sympathetic and recommended her for a situation as an assistant in a school for disabled children. Belinda was delighted, for it was what she had been training for and although she could not be in charge at the moment she was happy to work in a low position.

Stanley Brent meanwhile had been busy 'digging' into the past and had come up with some interesting information. He called to see Alfred and together they pieced together some of what must have occurred years ago.

Belinda had not been born in Wales but in a small town near Birmingham, nor was her father a coal Miner he was a Locksmith. "Ha" Alfred said. I see a pattern here, Yes Stanley agreed, and here it seems is the answer to why the 'Misses Jones' who by the way were then named 'Johns', left Birmingham. He placed a copy of a newspaper cutting on the table and waited for Alfred to read it. The headline read, 'THREE DARING RAIDS ON HIGH STREET BANKS' Alfred went on to read the article and whistled. Well a long stretch in prison would be worth the wait for that amount of money he exclaimed. I can imagine how unhappy they were to be released, only to discover that the whereabouts of their loot was lost to them. Considering how well the 'Ladies' had covered their tracks plus the name change I think the crooks did very well, to find them after all these years. Maybe the 'Force 'should employ them as detectives. Stanley jested. Perhaps we ought to tell the police of your findings. Alfred suggested. Don't worry, I already have. Stanley replied. Did they caution you for interfering in a police business? Alfred asked, with a smile. Something like that, Stanley laughed. But in less polite language.

Now that the police had completed their search of the cottage Belinda wanted to clear it all out, she had plenty of offers to help her and so 'The family' descended in force to begin the task .The skip outside the front door soon became full to over flowing and a second had to be ordered. I never thought that we had so much collected in such a small house. Belinda said stretching her aching back. Well you have been here twenty years. Beth said, and I dread to think how many needless belongings are in my room. Have these curtains got to come down or are you leaving them? She asked. I don't think they are good for anything but rags. Belinda replied. They even ripped out half the lining to see if anything was hidden there.

Right! Beth said, giving the curtains a hearty tug to draw them to one side, but as she did so she gave a startled cry for the whole lot fell upon her curtains, rails, and a good potion of plaster plus screws pulled away from the walls. Are you hurt? Belinda exclaimed rushing to her aid and trying to untangle her, while Beth coughed and choked with plaster dust. Oh dear, I've made another big hole in the wall. Beth said, I'm so sorry; she apologised. You can't make the mess any worse than it is already Belinda said. It's lucky that the lump didn't fall on your head. Don't worry I'm sure one of the workmen will plug it up again when they get here later. Belinda replied. As long as you're not hurt, that's the main thing. As Belinda began to assist Beth out of the tangled curtains she lifted a lump of plaster out of the way, glancing at it casually, and thinking it was a strange shape she remarked. This plaster looks as if there is something embedded in it. Have we got a hammer or anything that we could use to break it open? There is a poker in the fireplace said Beth I saw it just now That will do Belinda replied, and taking it she gave the plaster a hearty 'Whack' but after a few tries she gave up. Never mind Beth said. When the boys come they'll do it I'm sure, might as well let them do something useful. She rolled the old drapes into a ball and put them with the rest of the unwanted rags. After all that dust I think we deserve a cup of tea don't you? Belinda suggested going into the kitchen. As she switched on the kettle the 'boys' arrived. Trust them to arrive when it's 'tea and biscuit time'" Beth declared.

Donny followed Belinda into the kitchen. How have you been today? He asked looking at her keenly. You're not overdoing it are you? I'm fine, but there is something I would like you to do for me, Belinda said. Sure, anything. Donny replied. Thinking to him self there isn't anything I wouldn't do for you if only you gave me the right.

Belinda went into the other room and showed Donny the piece of plaster with what looked like a scrap of paper embedded into it. This isn't plaster. Donny said, inspecting the lump. It's cement, we need a heavy hammer, a fire poker's not strong enough, I'll ring Gramps he's got some tools he won't mind bringing something over.

Alfred when told of the find immediately said. Don't do anything until I come it might be something important, or even what the crooks were looking for. Within ten minutes Alfred arrived with his toolbox plus a heavy drill. What do you need all these tools for Gramps? Donny asked. Do- it- yourself has long been a hobby of mine. Alfred replied. I find it relaxing, and it's a good way of letting off steam if I have had a frustrating day. The arrival of Stanley was a surprise, but after Alfred had explained his presence they all settled down to the task in hand. With his powerful drill Alfred gently worked at the cement until it was nothing but crumbs and cement dust. At last the piece of delicate paper was freed and they all waited for Alfred to read it aloud. But it was written in code. What a disappointment. Stanley looking over Alfred's shoulder said   Wait a minute I know this code; we used to play it when we were kids and had secrets from our parents. I knew it was a good idea my asking you to come over. Alfred exclaimed. What does it say? For a minute Stanley perused the paper then and said. It doesn't say much just.' Look carefully under the tank'. What tank? Donny asked. I would guess it means the water tank in the roof, have you got a ladder? Stanley asked. There is a' built in' let down ladder inside the hatch lid. Belinda replied.

As one person they all trooped excitedly upstairs. Belinda explained how the ladder was brought down and soon Stanley was up in the roof space carefully treading on the joist's until he reached the water tank. Donny handed the torch from Alfred's toolbox up to him and they waited anxiously.

A few grunts and muttered 'words' were heard and then a triumphant "Gotcha "and Stanley's feet appeared from the hatchway onto the ladder once more. In his hand he carried a small square package wrapped in brown paper. Downstairs in the sitting room they all crowded round as Stanley carefully unwrapped the brittle paper and revealed a small book which proved to be a diary, written by Belinda's mother with all the happenings right from the beginning of the 'nightmare' situation which her little family had endured

From force of habit Stanley took a plastic sample bag from his pocket and carefully placed the book inside. Alfred suggested that they all go back to his house and Stanley could read the book to them in case some of it was written in 'the code'

This was agreed and excitedly they followed the two older men outside to the cars.

Seated comfortably on Rosamond's chintz covered chairs they waited eagerly for Stanley to read the diary. As the story unfolded they all became deeply engrossed in the happenings, and when it was finished Beth heaved a sigh. It would make a marvellous 'Film' she said.

When Rosamond returned from shopping the whole story had to be re –told, of how the crooks had devised a plan to rob three banks all at the same time, but they needed one more locksmith and Fred Johns was chosen, although he did not know them or who they were, they had told him they were customers who had a difficult lock that needed opening and he, thinking that it was a genuine job, agreed to do it. When he arrived to do the 'so called' job, they kidnapped him and threatened to kill his wife and child if he did not obey them. He refused and tried to run but they brought his wife and baby to the room where he was imprisoned and she begged him to do what they demanded. The plan was daring and successful as they raided three banks at once, it took only one man and one locksmith for each Bank all timed to be targeted at the same time.

It was not a large town and the police force was small. One of the gang telephoned the station pretending to be a panic-stricken bank employee who had overheard a plan to rob a completely different bank in another area. There were no mobile phones in those days and so by the time the bogus bank raid was discovered the actual raids had been committed and the crooks had gone off with the money. Fred Johns had tried to stop them but what could one man do against three determined men, and in their rush to get away they thrust him aside, he tripped and fell awkwardly, breaking his neck. They left him there at the scene and it was assumed at first that he was one of the gang, until Gweneth Johns told her side of the story and he was declared an innocent victim. She was able to tell the police who the men where and they were found, arrested and charged. The reward for their whereabouts and capture was given to Gweneth Johns and she and her baby disappeared from sight and sound. She changed their names and went to London, bought a house together with her sister and no more was heard of her. Hastily written at the end of the book was the destination of the stolen money.

For a moment there was silence before everyone began to talk at once, until Stanley held up his hand saying. If it's OK with you Belinda I'll take this book down to the station they'll be pleased with the break through, There's no need to tell you not to mention this to anyone outside this room, not even family at the moment. We have to keep it secret until these 'scum' have been caught.

They've waited twenty years to get their hands on this money, so they're not going to let anyone stand in their way now.

I'm sorry they wrecked your home Belinda but I'm sure the insurance will pay, and there may even be a reward from the three banks in a combined thank you, after all you lost your father when he was trying to save their money. And the information at the end of this book here may result in the recovery of most of it. He carefully put the re-wrapped book into his pocket and departed.

Alfred, entering his club one evening a few days later, met Stanley, who greeted him with "Just the man I want to see", I've an update for you on the 'Belinda ' case." Alfred at once motioned Stanley into the library where there were comfortable armchairs. They seated themselves and Stanley brought out a folder of papers. I have been doing some research of my own, he said, and it seems that two of the original bank robbers both died in prison, and the third man Gabby Small, after being released, went to live in the north of England. Moving about with no fixed address. He is known to Social Services and so I have been able to trace his movements. He is a heavy drinker and prone, when drunk, to boast of his exploits, his favourite being the story from years ago about the. Triple Bank Robberies. A young man heard his boastings, and had decided to see if he could locate the money. He questioned Gabby Small and discovered enough information for him to start making a search. As you know, if you have the knowledge and soft wear it's possible to find out anything these days however remote. This man, Sid Perkins, had both, especially the expertise. He set about tracing everything in the case and found that the Johns had changed their name and gone to London. Eventually he came up with the address. He discovered that much of the money had not been recovered and so he decided to find it for himself. His ransacking of the cottage was because Gabby Small had said that he was sure Gweneth Johns knew where it had been hidden. He was looking for clues; for he was sure that she would have wanted someone to know where it was .No doubt she had not expected to die so suddenly, before her daughter was old enough to be told. Goodness knows what she had intended to do with it, for she was an honest God fearing woman.

Sid Perkins was so determined to find any clues that when he went to the cottage expecting Belinda to be out at College, he had forgotten that the term had not started and she, unfortunately for her, was at home. He watched Donny leave and as soon as he was out of sight he went round to the back of the cottage. The back door was not locked and he was able to surprise Belinda, He attacked her brutally, bundled her into the shed, and must have clicked the lock. As you know he ransacked the house, but could find nothing. Any professional burglar would have searched the roof space and looked under the tank, it was one of the most obvious places, but he was not a 'Pro' just a 'Chancer'. He could have been a 'Murderer' too if Donny had not found Belinda in time.

He is now in prison awaiting trial for Assault and Battery, and Burglary with Intent, plus Criminal Damage. Alfred thumped his fist on the arm if his chair, saying angrily. I wish I were the Prosecuting Council for I would make sure that thug was sent down for the longest sentence possible.

I hope that they confiscate his computer, Stanley said, Otherwise I can see him organising a mass 'Break Out" from all the prisons in the country. It's a pity he doesn't use his expertise for something constructive instead of for crime.

CHAPTER FOUR

It's Belinda's birthday next week. Beth said. I didn't know that. Donny replied. I wonder if she would let me take her out for dinner to celebrate. I think it would be better if we all took her out, she'll be twenty-one. Beth replied. Why didn't she say anything about that? Donny asked in surprise. Of course she didn't, Beth said, you know what Belinda's like she would never push herself forward like that. Let's give her a surprise party then. Donny said eagerly. You girls can take her shopping and persuade her to get herself a new dress and a Hair do, I don't' think she would appreciate a surprise party if she had not had a chance to get herself ready. I'll book a nice private room in a Restaurant and give her a lovely time. Good idea. Beth said. She has been rather down since she learned of the reason for her father's death. She feels that she has missed so much by his being killed when he was so young.

What are you going to give Belinda for her birthday? Beth asked Donny. I thought that I would buy her some pearls, I noticed that she had a costume jewellery set which she was rather fond of but it broke and she lost most of the beads. Donny replied.

What about you? He asked. Oh I'll think of something pretty. Beth replied. Have you booked the venue yet? She asked. Yes it's all arranged including the band, all you girls have to do is turn up looking your usual charming selves Donny replied gallantly.

When the 'boys' arrived with their partners they were impressed with the arrangements made. 'Watch and learn!'' Donny declared, laughing, Next time it might be your turn.. Donny had collected Belinda, also Rosamond and Alfred who had been delighted to come with all the rest of the family it was a lovely and unexpected occasion for everyone. Donny had danced once or twice with Belinda but he claimed the last dance when the lights were lowered and the music slow and romantic. He couldn't resist holding her close with his lips closer, he whispered in her ear. You look lovely tonight Belinda. She smiled sweetly up at him saying. I guess it's the dress and 'Hair Do' Beth really went to town on me. You don't need a pretty dress and hairstyle to make you look lovely, you're always lovely in my eyes replied Donny. Mr Harris I've have told you before. Men like you eat girls like me for breakfast Thanks, but no thanks, Mr Harris. Belinda replied. How do you know you've said that to me before? Donny asked her. You know I did, I remember telling you when------- -She got no further for Donny had swept her into is arms hugging and kissing her. Do you realise that you have remembered something that happened weeks ago? It just popped into my head I don't know why Belinda said.

The dance had finished but they paused for a moment before hurrying over to Alfred and Rosalind. Donny said excitedly, Belinda has remembered something from weeks ago. How wonderful Rosamond exclaimed, I pray that this is the beginning of you're full recovery, my dear. Everyone crowded round with congratulations and 'Good Wishes', what a wonderful Twenty- first Birthday present. Beth exclaimed. A sentiment echoed by all.

Gradually each day Belinda began to regain a little of her memory, the doctor when visited, was hopeful of a full recovery for her. I'm glad that you have your memory coming back because now I can apologise for my behaviour when we first met, I wanted to tell you before, but when I went to the hotel to apologies, I found that you had gone. I was afraid to stay. Belinda explained. I 'm not very good at coping with men I must confess; I get very embarrassed and tongued tied. I thought you did very well at giving me a set down when you thought I needed it. Donny laughed. Was I rude? I suppose I was, I'm sorry. Belinda said. Well both of us have apologised, now can we be friends? Donny said, holding out his hand, which Belinda took, but instead of releasing her, Donny continued to hold her hand, and pulling her into his arms he kissed her. Are you going to slap my face now? Donny asked. But Belinda smiled and shook her head as she turned away.

Soon Belinda was able to go back to College and although she sometimes suffered a nightmare, her life became normal once more. But Donny still remembered the kiss he had given her at the party and planned to show Belinda that he was serious about her. He knew that she thought he was a' Play Boy' but that was in the past, now he had grown up and was ready to settle down, but how to convince Belinda of that he had no idea.

Donny often walked across the Park to his Grandparent's house he liked to 'keep an eye on them' for they were not 'getting any younger' as Alfred put it. Donny also hoped that he would see Belinda too on his visits. Today as he walked briskly over the grass he saw a little dog running too and fro sniffing at the ground, it seemed to be unaccompanied, ' I don't think there will be many rabbits here' thought Donny, but I'll bet a pound to a penny it's not rabbits that little tyke is looking for. At that moment a woman with a Poodle on a pink lead, came into the Park. Donny recognised them as the pair who had caused trouble before, from his distance he saw two dogs aiming for the same 'target' and he began to run towards them. The larger dog, a mongrel that had no collar, challenged the smaller dog, hackles raised, growling and snarling at each other, they were ready to fight. Suddenly, Donny recognised Pug who was the smaller dog. He shouted his name, but there was no response and swiftly removing his jacket he threw it over the little dog and swept him up in his arms away from the larger animal. Meanwhile ordering the woman to 'Take that blessed dog home, have you no sense madam, will you never learn to keep it in at such times, or else change it for a Male. And holding Pug up high so that the large dog could not reach him he strode away. Belinda, from a distance had seen what had happened, she had been searching for Pug who had escaped with one purpose in mind. It seems that the other dog had been roaming the park for some days and nobody knew where it came from. When she saw the way that Donny had saved Pug and without hesitation had ruined his expensive jacket, her doubts about him melted, for no dedicated 'Play Boy' would ruin his expensive clothing to protect an old lady's little dog. When Belinda came near she flung her arms about the dog and Donny, kissing him and saying breathlessly. Thank you so much you're an Angel. Well not yet I hope. Donny joked, returning her kiss. Good morning my love, come with me, I think we need to persuade Mrs Day that Pug needs to be taken to the Vet for 'obvious reasons', its not safe for either her or you to take him out in the park alone.

After that 'episode' Donny noticed that Belinda began to unbend towards him. If he complimented her about her appearance or any of her talents, she did not look at him as if he was not being sincere, and Donny began to feel more hopeful that maybe she would give him a chance to show her that he meant it when he finally managed to tell her how much he loved her.

Belinda was becoming more and more in love with Donny but she could not tell if Donny felt the same. He was always kind and considerate towards her but he was nice to Beth too. She did not see the loving looks that he gave her when she was not looking, but Beth noticed and urged him to let Belinda know how he felt, but he said that if he rushed her Belinda might draw back into her 'shell' once more and he could not bear the thought of that, and so matters stayed at a standstill, until one afternoon when Beth returned from college, she found them together in the cottage and Belinda was crying, because although she loved the cottage with all it's happy memories she felt that she could no longer live there and would have to sell it. Donny was looking distracted and not knowing what to do. When Beth arrived; she took in the situation at once and said impatiently. For Goodness sake Donny kiss the girl and tell her that you love her and will help her. You've both been 'in love' with each other for months and I'm tired of watching the pair of you stepping around each other and never getting anywhere. The 'Tragic pair' suddenly changed into the 'Happy pair' when they both realised that Beth was right. Proper little 'Match Maker' aren't you? Donny joked, hugging Beth, after he had hugged and kissed Belinda. I'm leaving now. Beth said. And the next time I see you both don't let me find that you haven't sorted everything out.

Yes Madame! Donny replied, saluting smartly. It shall be done; he finished with a cheeky grin. After Beth had gone Donny turned to Belinda and taking her hand he knelt on one knee amongst the builders rubble and said. Please, please, darling Belinda will you marry me? "Yes. Yes." she replied bending to hug and kiss him, and then chiding him. Look at your clothes; you're kneeling in the dust. Donny gave a mock sigh. Oh dear I'm in trouble already. He said with a grin. Let's go out now and buy the ring quickly, before you change your mind. He joked.

All the family were delighted to hear of the engagement. Janet telephoned Donny to warn him that he must abandon his 'Batchelor' ways from now on. You don't have to worry about that Mum. Donny assured her, when his mother had chided him. I know just how lucky I am to have a girl like Belinda loving me, and I would never do anything to hurt her or spoil our happiness.

CHAPTER FIVE

Beth and Belinda had been looking at wedding dresses, and as they left the Wedding Shop busily discussing the merits of the dresses they had seen, they heard music at the other end of the walkway. What's that? Beth said. Lets go and see Belinda suggested, tugging her arm. Come on! A small crowd had gathered and they worked their way to the front. An electric keyboard had been set up outside a music store and a young man was seated in front of it. A notice with the name of a well-known charity stood beside a bucket. As the girls arrived at the front of the crowd the young man began to play a popular song and some of the crowd good- naturedly joined in.

Marco Costa surveyed the crowd gathered round him and suddenly he noticed two attractive girls in the front. He thought that the girl with the blonde curls that framed a sweet face looked adorable and he wondered who they were. For some reason he began to play an old -fashioned Edwardian parlour song and he heard her companion say. That's Granny's favourite song she always asks you to sing it for her doesn't she? Marco rose from his seat and bowing to Beth, he took her hand and said. And now Signorina you shall sing it for me, 'Please?' He begged. Beth blushed and would have refused, but Belinda urged her. Go on Beth, it is for Charity after all. Beth reluctantly went to stand beside the keyboard and the young man asked in what key she would like to sing. He began to play and Beth forgetting her shyness began to sing. Her beautiful clear soprano voice echoed around the roof of the shopping arcade as if it were a cathedral, and when she had finished there was a moments silence before huge applause burst from the crowd and they asked for more, Beth sang two more songs and then she demurred saying, not quite truthfully, that she did not know any more songs and the crowd reluctantly dispersed, but not before putting quite a substantial amount of coins into the bucket.

Marco was thanking her profusely for her help, and Beth could tell by his accent that he was Italian, although his accent was slight it was very attractive and combined with his handsome face and tall athletic figure he was as Belinda had remarked earlier, 'Quite a Dish'. You must let me buy you a cup of tea. Marco insisted. After your help it's the least I can do. Beth was about to refuse, but Belinda said enthusiastically. That would be lovely, wouldn't it Beth? Then turning to Marco she added. We 've been shopping for Wedding Dresses all afternoon and we really need a break. Marco's heart sank and he thought 'Don't tell me that lovely girl is already spoken for' addressing Beth he asked. You are about to be married Signorina? Oh no, not me it's my friend here who's getting married. Beth replied. Privately relieved Marco said. Congratulations Signorina. Come, we shall go for tea and get acquainted. And waving them to go before him followed them across to the little teashop opposite.

Comfortably seated at a corner table, and after they had placed their order, Marco introduced himself, he told them He was Marco Costa his Mother was English his father Italian and he now lived and worked in London. That is enough about me. He said. What about you? He asked Beth. How is that you sing like an Angel? Hardly like an Angel Beth replied. But I am at College studying Singing, Piano and Violin. Ah, now I understand he said, and turning to Belinda he said. What about you Signorina are you at the Music College too? Yes, she replied, I'm going to teach music and singing in a school for disabled children. I'm getting married in a few weeks time but I won't finish College until next year, I'm Belinda by the way and this is Beth. Marco solemnly shook hand with both of the girls but his eyes were laughing, one of the things Beth had first notice about him, he had lovely expressive eyes. What time do you finish College? Marco asked. About four o'clock Beth said. Bene! Will you let me take you both out to dinner tomorrow night? He asked. Both the girls looked doubtful. I'm sorry; you don't know me do you? It is right that you should be careful, but I promise you I am harmless, I would never hurt you. Beth will go wont you? Belinda replied, Donny and I are house hunting. Will you come Beth? Marco asked. But Beth still looked doubtful. Belinda nudged Beth in the ribs with her elbow, and whispered.'Say yes'. And so at last Beth smiled shyly and nodded. Yes, and thank you for the invitation.

When Marco called to take Beth out, she was not quite ready and her mother, Anna, invited him in to wait for her. She was pleasantly surprised for she had been concerned and wondered if a young man who would invited a young girl to dinner after meeting her so causally in the Shopping Mall could be a reliable person, and she asked him several searching questions

Beth and Marco spent a pleasant evening together getting to know each other and the more they learned the more comfortable they felt together and by the end if the evening they both said that it seemed as if they had been friends for years. Maybe we knew each other in another life, Beth thought, it certainly felt that way to her.

When Marco reluctantly took Beth home she asked him if he would like to meet her father, for she had seen him looking from the window as soon as Marco's car had drawn up outside the house. I'm sorry to subject you to so much parental scrutiny, Beth apologised. Marco smiled, I understand, he replied. If my Papa had a daughter as lovely as you he would have insisted on coming with us. Your Papa is right to be careful of you. I would be the same. I'll call you tomorrow. He said as he left after his brief visit.

When Marco had left Beth asked her mother. What do you think Mum? He's a lovely man, but don't get too fond of him just yet darling. Anna replied. You don't know him very well or his background; charming men aren't always what they seem. I hope for you're sake that he is genuine, I would be happy for you if he is.

Meanwhile Marco was thinking on similar lines he was

very drawn to Beth and knew that he could easily fall in love with her, but he had been hurt before when he was a very young man and he was a little wary.

As he entered the room in the Hotel where he was staying, his mobile rang, it was his mother calling to say that his father was very ill and would he come at once. Before leaving, he wrote a note to Beth explaining the situation, and containing his address and telephone number in Italy, he left this at the Reception Desk to be stamped and posted.

Beth heard no more from Marco, and although she was extremely disappointed she did not show it or say anything about it, she made up her mind to forget about the handsome heartbreaker as soon as possible. This resolution however was easier said that done for she felt very hurt by his treatment. Belinda was indignant that anyone should treat her friend so casually, but Beth was busy at college with final exams and she set aside her 'woes' to concentrate on her work.

CHAPTER SIX

When Marco landed in Milan, he went directly from the Airport to the Hospital, His father had suffered a serious heart attack, and had been given a delicate operation, and was now in intensive care, for the surgeon had done all he could and the rest, as the Doctor said, was up to the strength of Benito's constitution and God's will. Marco and his mother took turns at watching by Benito's bed almost non- stop and Marco was there when his father regained consciousness. What are you doing here my son, who is looking after the business? Were the first words he uttered? Marco was so relieved to hear that his father was 'back in the world' that he almost laughed. But instead he replied. So Papa you have decided that you will stay with us after all. Of course his father replied, smiling. Who else would keep you 'in line' my son? Marco gave his father a gentle hug. What a fright you gave us Papa, but you will get better now. Yes? The doctor appeared followed by Signora Costa, and Marco moved out of the ward so that he could text his office with the good news. Benito's condition improved rapidly each day and soon he was fit enough to go home.

While he had been absent Marco and Angela had re-arranged many things in the Villa so that it was more suited for someone whose heart was weak, and at last Benito was able to go home but with strict instructions not to overwork himself.

Now that his father was on the mend Marco began to prepare for his return to London. He had been in regular contact with his office and his secretary had found the address of a suitable flat, which she had viewed and tentatively reserved for him.

When Rosamond had married Alfred, she found that her dead husband's Will had stated that she could not sell the house and so she had converted it into two self - contained flats. Donny lived in the ground floor flat and the one above was at present empty, the previous occupant having returned to Australia.

Marco decided that this afternoon was a good time to go and check out the 'apartment'. When he arrived, Donny was about to leave and greeted him as a new neighbour, they spoke for a few moments and Donny excused himself, saying that he was off to meet his fiancée and with a wave of his hand he was gone. Marco liked the flat, it was comfortably furnished and bright most of all it was spotlessly clean. He decided that he would go to the agent and finish all arrangements before he collected his belongings from his temporary room at the hotel.

Donny told Belinda that he had met the new upstairs neighbour who seemed a nice chap, Belinda was curious for more details such as. What did he look like, is he married, what is his job? " I don't know" were Donny's answers to all of these questions, much to Belinda's disappointment.

Rosamond had asked Beth if she would mind just checking that the cleaning firm had properly cleaned the flat, because a new tenant would soon be taking it. Beth was happy to be of help and said that she would go on the way home from college. When she arrived she noticed a car that she had not seen before, standing in the driveway. 'That must be the new tenant' she thought. At that moment the door opened and a man descended the front steps, Beth looked at him curiously and received a huge shock, it was Marco. She turned quickly away intending that he should not see her, but it was too late and he called out. Beth please, don't run away, wait a moment. Reluctantly Beth turned and waited for him to come nearer. Hello Marco. She said coldly. Marco was puzzled, what had happened to make Beth so distant to him, what had he done? If you'll excuse me I have to do an errand for my friend. She said and turning away she hastily went into the downstairs flat and closed the door. Marco stood there for a moment feeling stunned, and then he felt angry. Why was she treating him so, what had he done?

He couldn't stay now, but he was determined that he would find out before too long.

Beth waited until she saw Marco drive away and then she went home. She didn't say anything about her meeting with Marco, she felt too upset. For she now knew that she cared for him more that she had realised.

Marco settled into the flat. At first he had considered looking for another, but this one was conveniently situated for his work and he liked the area, plus he was determined to find out why Beth was behaving so strangely. He discovered in conversation with Donny that Belinda was his fiancée and that they were to be married in a few weeks time. He told Donny of his meeting with Belinda and Beth, and Donny laughed. Yes the girls told us about that, poor Beth was really embarrassed at the time, I don't know why because she has a beautiful singing voice. Granny always says it makes her want to cry it's so lovely. Marco didn't mention Beth, for he had decided to wait and see what developed, for he was sure that he and Beth had both been attracted to each other and something must have happened while he was away 'please don't let it be another man 'he thought. But when he met Belinda again even she was stiff and coldly polite to him, not at all like the friendly smiling girl she had been before. It must be something that I have done to upset them both he thought, but what could it have been? Perhaps he should ask Belinda, but he did not want to offend her since his flat was so close to Donny's it could prove awkward.

Beth had not told her mother that Marco was living in the flat above Donny for she knew that Anna would warn her not to become too attached to him. She had given herself this advice often, but it did not seem to help, and this was one reason why she did not want to meet him again, although she knew that it was bound to happen with Donny living close by, so that unless she refused to visit Belinda until they moved to a new house she would have to meet Marco again before long.

The meeting happened sooner than she had thought it

would, for she went to Donny's flat to collect some papers for her father who was in court that day and he needed the papers which Donny had taken away, by mistake, with some of his own. As Beth left Donny's flat the upstairs door opened and Marco descended the steps. He smiled and said. How lovely to see you, I was going to call and ask you if I could take you out to dinner. I'm really busy this week. Beth replied stiffly. What about next week? Marco asked. I'm afraid I'm busy then too. Beth replied. When will you be free? Marco persisted, taking out his diary. We could make a date for when you're available. I don't know when that will be and I don't have my diary with me. Beth answered vaguely. I must go, goodbye. As she turned away, Marco called. Can I give you a lift anywhere? But Beth did not answer and hurried away. Something is very wrong here, Marco thought, perhaps I should ask Donny if he has any idea what it can be. He had to go up to Birmingham on business and decided that he would go tomorrow, he was obviously not going to get any answers from Beth or Belinda but he was determined that he would get them from somebody no matter how long it took.

Beth told Belinda of the meeting, she was sympathetic but was of the opinion that perhaps being an Italian and so charming he was just being himself and had not meant to give her a wrong impression. Beth thought that was probably the answer and promised herself to be more cautious in future.

Donny, being unaware of Beth's problem with Marcus was willing to include him in their circle of friends, and Beth found that every time they were all together Marco was included in the group. She began to feel the strain and soon began to refuse invitations from Belinda and Donny to join them and other friends. At last after several weeks of Beth's continued excuses Belinda complained. We never seem to see you these days, you're always busy or feeling unwell. Are you overdoing the study? You know that you'll easily pass all your exams you're so talented.

Oh I'm fine, don't worry about me, you have to concentrate on you're wedding preparations. How are they going by the way? Belinda soon forgot her intention to 'sort Beth out' and launched into her description and explanations, Beth had managed to divert her this time.

CHAPTER SEVEN

Anna had noticed Beth's listless manner and mentioned it to Drew. Oh you know how young girls are, he said. If they're not unwell, they're in love or have too many late nights. Beth hasn't had a late night for ages, in fact she doesn't seem to have been out at all lately now that I come to think of it. Anna said. Well love, the best way to find out is to ask her what's the matter. Drew replied. I've tried that. Anna explained, but she always says nothing is wrong. Then it must be unrequited love. Drew joked returning to his newspaper. Anna thought about this, in spite of his joke Drew could be right. She began to watch Beth and noticed that she never went to a party or anywhere that she might meet Donny, what had she got against her cousin? They had always got on well together in spite of the age gap. When he was asked, Drew replied. Maybe it's not Donny but somebody or the company he keeps that Beth doesn't like.

Anna asked Belinda who usually went out with them these days. Oh the usual crowd, but just lately Marco often comes too since he lives in the same house and Donny seems to like him. Belinda said dismissively. Don't you like Marco then? Anna asked. Yes he's OK, and he has plenty of charm, but I don't think he's very sincere, well he wasn't with Beth anyway. In what way was that? Anna asked casually, she felt that she was near to getting an answer to Beth's problem, but she had to be careful or Belinda would guess that she was probing, and loyalty to Beth would silence her. Well you see, Belinda continued, feeling that at last she could confide in Anna without feeling that she was telling tales. When we first met Marcus in the shopping centre, and he took Beth out to Dinner he was so charming and attentive that he seemed totally attracted to Beth as much as she was to him. He made arrangements to take her out again but he didn't turn up, and she saw and heard nothing of him for three months.

Then he turned up renting the flat above Donny and trying to date her again. Each time she makes an excuse he asks her again and she is running out of excuses, and so she avoids him. But since he and Donny seem to be 'Best Buddies' at the moment that is rather difficult and so she doesn't come with us. He really hurt her by his behaviour you know, and I don't blame her for avoiding him. Belinda was relieved to have been able to tell Anna what had been worrying her for some time. Thank you for telling me. Anna said. I have been puzzled by her behaviour but now I understand. Anna thought about Beth's disappointment and wondered if there was a way that she could help, she did not want to interfere, but she could see how unhappy her daughter was and she longed to do something about it.

As it happened she did not have to do anything about the problem for one afternoon there was ring on the doorbell and when she opened the door it was Marco. Could I speak with you please Mrs Parry? He asked politely. Of course, do come in, Anna replied, leading the way into the sitting room.

I am sorry to trouble you Mrs Parry, but I was wondering if you would help me. Marco said. I'll help you if I can, but what's troubling you so much?

You know that I took Beth out to dinner when we first met don't you? He asked. Yes, and Beth was very happy about it too. Anna replied. Yes, he said, that is what I thought, but since I have come back to London she won't have anything to do with me and shuns my company at all times. She makes excuses not to join her group of friends, I know it is because of me and I don't understand what it is that I have done, he finished, and looked so sad that Anna felt drawn to him in a motherly way.

What made you leave London? Anna asked? My Papa was seriously ill, he had a heart operation and we did not think he would live, I stayed with my Mama to support her, I have no sisters or brothers and she has only me to comfort her. We sat by Papa's bed in turns for many weeks, he is still weak but is now at home, and I have come back to run the business, I don't suppose that my Papa will ever be well enough to travel far again and so I must take his place. He replied.

Did Beth know that you had to go at once to be with your parents at such a traumatic time? Anna asked. Oh yes, I wrote to her explaining it all, I left a letter at the Hotel Reception for them to stamp and post. Marco replied. Well, as far as I know Beth didn't receive any letter from you about your dreadful worries, if she had, she would've told me I'm sure of that. She would have been concerned for you, and I know that she would've contacted you to give her support Anna said.. How did you know where to send the letter? Anna asked. I sent it here to number seventy-five. Marco replied. But we are number fifteen. Anna said. You must have misread the number in the dark, there is no number seventy-five, the road isn't long enough for that many houses.

Now I see what has been the matter with Beth, she thought that you went away without telling her, because you weren't serious about your friendship with her, and you stayed away for three months without a word. Did you send other letters too? Yes of course you did, and none of them reached us for there is no such address. What a mess, but never mind now you will be able to explain it all, and be sure you make her listen, now off you go, she has gone to Donny's flat to tidy up and to be alone too I guess. She spends a great deal of time alone lately, but I'm sure that you'll soon change that, Anna said, smiling at him. Marco took Anna's hand and kissed it. I salute you Signora thank you so much. Then he was gone, and jumping into his car he sped away. Anna hoped he wouldn't get a ticket for speeding.

Marco could hardly wait to get to Donny's flat and explain everything to Beth. At the flat he 'leant' on the bell and it rang long and loudly. Inside the flat, Beth who was washing up her coffee cup jumped and dropped the cup into the sink where its handle promptly fell off. Oh bother, she muttered, just wait till I speak to that idiot at the door, and marching into the hallway she opened the door saying. Do you have to make such a racket, you made me break a cup, and what's so urgent anyway? Then realising it was Marco she said .Oh I might have known it would be you, and she began to close the door, but Marco putting his arm between the door and the doorframe said calmly. Unless you wish to break my arm Signorita I suggest that you allow me to speak, for I am not so easily deterred. OK 'Speak' but hurry up I'm busy. Beth replied tersely. Ah, Cara Mia, such a hard heart for a lady with such a pretty face. Marco replied smiling tenderly at her. May I not come in? He queried still smiling, for she reminded him of a little hen whose feathers had been ruffled in the rain.

Reluctantly Beth opened the door wide and stood aside to allow Marco to enter. Marco sketched a mock bow and walked past her into the sitting room. Beth stood with her arms folded defensively, waiting for Marco to speak, and when he did, she was amazed and ashamed at her behaviour towards him. When he had at last finished his complete explanation, she burst into tears sobbing I'm so, so sorry Marco I should have trusted you until I had heard the whole reason for your absence. I've made us both miserable for nothing but a mistake. No 'Amore' it is not all your fault we must share the blame for I stupidly sent my letters to the wrong address, I should have realised that the road was not long enough for seventy five houses. But my only excuse is that I was trying so hard not to sweep you into my arms and kiss you as I longed to do, but I have no reason not to do so now, and he folded her tightly in his arms, kissing her repeatedly until they were both breathless.

Have you finished in here? He asked. I want us to go back and see your Mama, she has been so kind to me, for she allowed me to explain to her what had happened, and sent me here to speak with you, if she had not we would still be miserable would we not Cara? Why do you call me, 'Cara' my name is 'Beth' she said. It means 'sweetheart' would you prefer I did not call you that? Marco asked, Oh no, it makes me feel 'special' I love it. Beth replied, shyly putting her arms round his neck and kissing him. There was no conversation for a while, until Marco said, Basta! Enough! You are making my head spin, come little one we will go and tell your Mama that we are 'affianced 'What does that mean? Beth asked. It means we will be married soon. Marco replied, smiling broadly. But you haven't asked me yet Beth said in surprise. First I have to get permission from your Papa, Marco explained. Beth laughed. You're so sweet and 'old fashioned' and I love you for it, but darling Marco we don't have to do that in England anymore. I would still like to ask him anyway, he might not approve of me. Marco replied.

Unknown to the happy pair, Drew had already checked on Marco and his family, for although he might appear not to have had much concern about Beth's relationships, he was in fact a very protective father, although his children were not aware of that.

Belinda when told the happy news was thrilled, and apologetic to Marco, I'm so, so, sorry, I didn't know of the mix up either she said, after Marco had explained. You were being loyal to your friend, and that is good. He replied I would welcome such a good friend too maybe? He asked smiling. Yes, 'Friends' agreed Belinda giving him a hug.

The engagement ring was chosen and duly presented to Beth by Marco, and a small family 'Dinner Party' was held to mark the occasion. They had not wanted any big fuss and were happy to let Belinda and Donny's wedding take centre stage.

As the Wedding Day drew near Belinda began to get nervous. Supposing it rained or was very cold or one of them were ill until at last Donny protested. Enough with the gloom and doom anyone would think you don't want to get married. It's not that, Belinda protested. It's just that

I want it all to be perfect. Of course it will be perfect, it won't matter what the weather is like, or if one of us is ill. If I were in my 'Hospital Bed' I would still marry you no matter what. So cheer up my love or I will begin to think you are hoping that a disaster will stop us from getting married. It's not going to, so stop worrying.

At last the Wedding Day arrived the weather was mild, bright and sunny nobody was ill, everything went off splendidly, and the happy couple were waved off to the Airport to begin their Honeymoon in an unknown destination. It had to be a secret because it I was a surprise for Belinda. Donny was taking her somewhere she had always wanted to go; she was taking her camera and had promised to take plenty of photos.

After the excitement of Belinda and Donny's wedding, life became less frantic. Drew and Anna had welcomed Marco into the family but they had asked that he and Beth waited a while before marrying, not because they did not like him, but because they felt that he and Beth had not known each other long enough. Reluctantly the young pair agreed, and when Marco's parent's gave them exactly the same advice, they settled down to get to know each other better, and as Anna said, Enjoy you're freedom before the responsibilities of married life are upon you.

CHAPTER EIGHT

Jonathan Parry gazed dolefully at the large pile of briefs on his desk, thinking It's good to have work but one can have too much of a good thing, and giving a sigh he applied himself once more to the closely written sheets of paper.

He really missed Mrs Brown since she had retired, for she had always been there to help him ever since he had been a 'raw recruit' of a young solicitor who knew almost nothing about the complications of working in a prestigious law practice, except what he had learned in University and that didn't help him much. Mrs Brown had spoilt them all including his grandfather, uncle and father. Since her leaving there had been a succession of young women calling themselves 'Legal Secretaries' all glamorous with plenty of make up, and plenty of hair but it seemed very little knowledge of how to be a 'legal secretary.' Jonathan sighed once more and reluctantly pressed the buzzer for the latest 'secretary' to come into his office

There was a tap on the door and at his brief "Come in" the door opened, Jonathan looked up and did a double take. What are you doing here? He asked in amazement. Mrs Brown recommended me to Mr Alfred, the girl replied. And he actually employed you? Does he know everything? If you mean does he know that I was expelled from University for cheating in my exams, yes he does know and he believed me when I told him the whole of the circumstances. He knows it wasn't me, but it's no good expecting you to believe me. She said bitterly beginning to leave. But she heard her Grandfather's voice in her head saying. 'You're innocent girl, stand up for yourself; don't let anyone get you down.' And so instead of leaving as she had intended she turned back and said. If you want to sack me you will have to go to your Grandfather for he was the one who employed me. And once more she prepared to leave the room. Wait! Jonathan ordered, since you're here you might as well make yourself useful, he said ungraciously. Ingrid Andres looked at him contemptuously for a moment and then turned back into the room and stood beside his desk. What is it that needs attention? She asked.

It's these papers they're in a devil of a mess, Mrs Brown always dealt with this and I don't have time to sort them out, I have to be in court shortly and I need some of them to take with me, 'Typical man, Ingrid thought, leaving everything to the last minute', and she swiftly sorted through the papers retaining those he would need immediately, the others she took away to file. Jonathan unwillingly surprised at her efficiency, took his brief case and departed.

That evening he thought about the situation at work with Ingrid, he didn't know what to believe, the evidence had all pointed to her guilt, but if his grandfather believed her story, perhaps he ought to rethink his own opinion. The next day when he arrived at the chambers he found Ingrid already at work. She had cleared his desk, had filed away unnecessary files and on his desk had laid all appropriate files for today's court hearings. He had to admit that things were running much as it had when Mrs Brown had been there.

How are you getting on with Miss Andres? Alfred asked, when he and Jonathan went out to lunch. Why do you ask? Jonathan replied. Oh I wondered if she was as efficient as Mrs Brown hoped she would be, his Grandfather said, looking at him enquiringly. Jonathan felt uncomfortable for he knew that Alfred was aware of Ingrid's past and that he also knew of Jonathan's opinion when it came to the truth of that history. Have you ever thought that you might have judged Ingrid wrongly? And aren't you just a little 'doubtful' that you are entirely right? Alfred persisted. Are you wearing your Magistrates hat now? Jonathan asked. Well a little, his grandfather said. I think that looking at both sides of the case might not be a bad idea my Boy. Did you ever try to get at the truth, or did you just take the word of others, and how are you going to feel when I uncover the truth and you find that you were wrong? Alfred queried, looking at him sternly. It was five years ago, what 's the use of trying to find out now? Jonathan replied. If it were you who had been wrongly accused and punished, I would not think that twenty years was too late to clear your name my Boy, and that is how Mrs Brown feels about her granddaughter. Alfred chided him. I didn't know that she was Mrs Brown's relation. Jonathan said, frowning. She didn't tell me. Why would she tell you anything, she knows that you think she is a liar and a cheat and would not believe her claim. You should try to be more flexible in your opinions you know, it doesn't do to think that you are always in the right, there are two sides to every story and I think that you would do well to remember that. Alfred said severely.

Back in the office Jonathan thought about what his grandfather had said, he didn't often chide any of his family but when he did it was always for a good reason. Perhaps I should listen to what Ingrid has to say and not make a snap judgement. I've never properly heard her side of the story; I'll start as soon as she comes in tomorrow, before we begin work.

The next morning Jonathan came prepared with notes and a list of questions he wanted to ask Ingrid. He must be tactful when he asked questions. I don't want to upset her and make her leave, he thought, for in truth he had come to look forward to seeing her each morning, she seemed to bring the 'Sunshine' with her and even on a dull day she brightened the office with her Nordic blonde hair and bright blue eyes., and she was always cheerful and polite.

Would you tell me something Ingrid? He asked. Would you explain to me exactly what happened at the University? And why did they accuse a respectable girl like you with the incident. Ingrid shook her head. You wouldn't believe me if I told you. She replied. Let me be the judge of that. Jonathan said. I'm not going to accuse you of lying, but what I want to find out is who it was that made all this trouble for you, and why. You know that I nearly failed my exams because of it don't you? So I would like to get to the bottom of the mystery too. Have you any suspicion as to who it could have been?

Ingrid paused for a moment as if collecting her thoughts. I always thought that it was Archie Forbes. She said. Archie! Why would you think that? He always seemed a decent chap Jonathan said.

If you were a girl you wouldn't think so. Ingrid replied. He was a 'little worm and a sleaze' like a lot of small men he had a giant ego and thought himself irresistible to the girls. I rejected him several times and he vowed he would show me who was boss. I thought he meant to get me alone one night and so I avoided him as often as possible. But he was too clever to try anything against the law; his speciality was 'plotting' situations where people would get into trouble for something that they had 'appeared' to have done when really it was his doing. Wow, that was some smart deduction on your part. Jonathan said admiringly. But what made you so sure that it was Archie?

Something about the way he acted and remarks that he made. He had that 'I told you so' expression on his face when he said to me. 'Who's the Boss now?' and 'Not so clever as you thought were you? She said. But that could just have been jeering at you. Jonathan replied. Yes, that was what I thought at first. Ingrid said. But when all your notes and your 'dissertation' disappeared just before your exams I knew that this must be more than a mistake Archie was always jealous of you, you know, we all thought that his jokes and poking fun at you was only banter, but I'm pretty sure that he meant it all seriously. His room was next to yours wasn't it? She asked. Yes but I had locked the door. Jonathan replied. Ingrid laughed, Didn't you know that most of the keys fitted most of the doors, in that block, I know because often if we couldn't find our own key we would borrow one from somebody else. I wish I'd known that it would have been jolly useful.

Jonathan said. Ingrid laughed. Didn't your big sister teach you anything before you went to UNI? No, because my' big sisters' did not go to University they went to a Dance and Drama College Jonathan replied grinning. But I'll bet they would have told me if they had known. We were triplets and always into mischief together as kids. Are you really a triplet? Ingrid said intrigued. I've never known a triplet before. Yes it was great; we always stuck up for each other in all our scrapes. Jonathan replied. You were lucky then, all my 'big brother 'ever did was over - protect me. He is ten years older than I am, and takes things very seriously, I used to tell him he was no fun at all, I must have been a trial to him. She said.

Have you told my grandfather of your suspicions about Archie Forbes? Jonathan asked. Yes, and he seems to think that it could be the answer, but proving it would be difficult. She replied. Well, Jonathan said. I'm sorry that you weren't able to finish your Law Degree but I'm pleased that you became a Legal Secretary otherwise you wouldn't be here would you? Why Mr Harris, was that a compliment by any chance? Ingrid said in a fake American accent. Why yes Miss Andres, I believe it was. Jonathan replied mimicking her accent in return.

Now that the air had been cleared between them, Jonathan thought at first that he could settle down and forget about the whole incident. But somehow it niggled at his conscience that Archie Forbes had ruined Ingrid's career and had not been made to pay for his sins. He had discussed it with his grandfather who seemed to feel that the matter was closed, but Jonathan could not let it go.

When they were not too busy with work, Jonathan and Ingrid often went out for lunch together. One lunch time as they had settled at their usual table a tall dark haired man entered the restaurant, and Ingrid seeing him waved and motioned him to come over to them, saying. Hello darling, come and sit with us. When the man bent to kiss Ingrid. Jonathan felt a twinge of jealousy, which surprised him, and made him realise that he was getting very attached to

Ingrid and looked forward to being alone with her. The stranger was seated at their table and Ingrid introduced him. This is Karl. She said. He is a Detective Inspector with the Met. That must be a more interesting job than being a Solicitor. Jonathan remarked. Oh it has its moments. Karl replied smiling, every job has its highs and lows I guess, you might say we catch them and you dispatch them. Jonathan grinned. Very well put he replied.

Lunch proved to be better than Jonathan had thought it would be for Karl was an interesting conversationalist and made them laugh at some of the incidents that he had encountered while a young recruit. Looking at his watch, Karl said. As much as I have enjoyed your company, I have to leave I'm afraid, duty calls. Yes it's time we went too. Jonathan replied rising and holding Ingrid's coat for her to slip it on, she thanked him and then turning, gave Karl a hug and a kiss, saying. I'll see you tonight love, and she waved as he walked away.

Jonathan felt as if the bottom had dropped out of his world as he realised with a shock that he didn't want Ingrid to be 'In love' with anyone else, he wanted her to love him as much as he loved her. He was very quiet all afternoon working on a difficult case, at last Ingrid asked him. Don't you feel well Jonathan? Why do you ask? He said. You've been so quiet all afternoon is something worrying you. Is there a problem with this case? Ingrid asked. Something is worrying me but I'm not sure you will want to hear it. Jonathan answered. Try me, you might be surprised, I can be sympathetic. Ingrid laughed.

Jonathan began to look harassed and suddenly Ingrid stopped laughing and became concerned. Now you're worrying me Jonathan please tell me. She begged. Jonathan took a deep breath, then said, I'm feeling jealous of that chap who had lunch with us, I'm in love with you Ingrid and I know I don't have a chance because he is taller and better looking than me. For a moment Ingrid was silent and then she put her arms around him and hugged him. Darling Jonathan I thought you'd never say it; I've been longing to hear you say that you feel the same as I do. Jonathan stared at her for a moment then hugged and kissed her in return.

After a while Ingrid said. I thought you would have guessed that he was my brother, not a 'boy friend'. How would I guess that, he looks nothing like you, he is dark and you are so fair? Jonathan said. Yes, he looks like my mother and I take after my father. My grandfather came from Sweden during the Second World War to join the British Army and after the war he stayed here and married my grandmother. She had dark hair, hence the different in our colouring. Ingrid explained. I'll take you to meet my family and you'll see for yourself. Do you think they will like me? He asked anxiously. What's not to like? Ingrid replied, smiling at him fondly. Let's go and tell Gramps and Dad about us. Jonathan said eagerly. Alfred and Seb Harris were not at all surprised at their news, they had suspected for some time that Jonathan and Ingrid were unaware of their feelings for each other, and much to their relief they had now finally realised it for themselves. You are going to marry me aren't you? Said Jonathan anxiously as they both slid into his car. Oh yes, just let anyone try and stop me. Ingrid replied, and Jonathan smiled broadly as he started his car and prepared to drive her home.

CHAPTER NINE

Jonathan still could not forget about the false accusations against Ingrid that had caused her to be unfairly dismissed from University and to be labelled a liar and a cheat. He was determined that he would find out who it was that had caused Ingrid to be shamed in such a way. Occasionally a group of his old classmates gathered for a 'get together' evening, usually he did not bother to go. But the next time I will, thought Jonathan, and so when Bill Simms rang to tell him of the next meeting he agreed to meet at the usual venue.

When Jonathan arrived at the Pub his old student friends greeted him with pleasure. Although he was not a drinker he accepted a glass of Lager and settled down to hear all their news. What about you Jonno? Bill asked. How do you like it working in the family business?

Well I suppose it was a bit boring at first, but now I'm being given my own clients and its much better. Jonathan replied. Rather you than me. Bill said. I'd go mad if I had to work with my Old Man he'd be on at me all the time, he's such a fussy old stick. I like working with Gramps and Dad. Jonathan replied. They never got impatient with me when I first started and even now that I have my own clients, I can always ask them if I need advice. In fact we sometimes have a conference about our respective cases, it's often a help to talk things over.

Well I never, a voice behind him exclaimed. Well, if it isn't the 'Teacher's Pet'? You don't often grace us with your presence. Jonathan recognised that sneering voice and turning round he greeted Archie Forbes with a grin. Hello 'Archibald' so you're still at liberty then, thought you would have been deported by now, he joked. No such luck. Archie replied, but I could do with a holiday. Jonathan thought that Archie did not look well, his face was pasty and his hand shook as he raised his glass, not a glass of beer Jonathan noted, but spirits. No wonder his hand shakes he thought and wondered why he had not realised before that Archie was a heavy drinker, how had he managed to pass his law exams if his brain was clouded with drink, they were difficult enough when sober but must be impossible half drunk. What if it had been Archie, as Ingrid suspected, who had taken the exam papers and then after reading them for himself he had placed them in Ingrid's room, it would have been safer than taking them back to the office and also would 'pay her back' for rejecting him. He must try to trick Archie into revealing his guilt, but 'How' that was the problem.

As the evening wore on Archie became more and more tipsy, while they were playing darts he almost impaled one of the other customers with a wildly thrown dart and had to be relegated to being in charge of the scoreboard. He went through various stages, first of all he was 'jolly' insisting on buying drinks all round even for those people he did not know, then he became 'argumentative' and finally he became 'maudlin'. Bemoaning that no one liked him, because his father was a Judge and they thought that he would get special treatment at college, and then saying that his father had always nagged him to get high grades in all his exams especially in university, he hated law and knew that he would never pass the exams. But his father wanted him to be a Judge too when he was older.

On and on he mumbled and very little notice was taken of his ramblings, until he laughed and said. You all thought so much of that 'Teacher's Pet' Jonno he never had any trouble learning his laws, and that' Stuck up Tart' Ingrid Andres too, but I fixed her, good and proper when I took the envelope of exam questions, and after I had read them I put them in her room and' Teachers Pet's 'dissertation and notes as well, he would have failed his exams if some busybody hadn't found them all, before it was too late. But she got expelled for cheating Ha! Ha! The best of the joke is that it was me who did the cheating in the exams and she got the blame. A stunned silence held the room for a moment before there were gasps of shocked exclamations from the others, and when Jonathan turned to them and asked. Would any one be agreeable to testify to what Archie has just confessed? There was a hundred percent "Yes" from all of them.

Archie was still boasting of his exploit saying how clever he had been to get unseen into the dean's office and steal the papers. Jonathan telephoned his father, and Seb said that he would come at once for he viewed it as a serious matter. He arrived shortly after, bringing Alfred, his father, with him and very soon statements had been taken from everyone who had heard what Archie had confessed. Archie was by now asleep but Seb and Alfred hustled him into Seb's car and took him back to his father's house where they explained what had happened and Archie's crime.

Judge Forbes could not believe that Archie had done such a mean trick on his class mates, he had known that Archie was struggling to pass his exams, but he never thought that his son would stoop so low as to cheat and let someone else take the blame.

The next morning Archie had sobered up and although his head ached abominably he was able to talk with his father and admitted that it was all-true, he had taken the papers and used them to cheat before putting them into Ingrid's room along with Jonathans Dissertation and notes. But how did you get hold of the papers in the first place. His father asked. Oh it was easy I just picked the locks. Archie replied. What do you mean, you 'picked the locks' only a criminal can do that they were special locks. I learned to pick locks when I was ten years old. Archie replied. Where on earth did you learn to do that, not at school I hope,? His father asked. "No" Archie replied. It was at home; do you remember we had a gardener called Seth? He was an ex- safe breaker, and a really interesting man, I never had anyone to play with and so I would go down to the potting shed and sit with Seth, he would tell me all sorts of tales about his exploits, I realise now that most of them weren't true, but he did know how to pick really complicated locks, he had a box of them and he taught me all about them and how to open them without anyone knowing you had done it. His father groaned. All that money spent on your Education and the most difficult thing you learned to do was pick locks.

You are in trouble now my boy, your degree will be taken away and you could even face prison for obtaining it for falsifying the results. Archie said nothing, for he did not know how to make it up to his father for what he had done, he realised how stupid he had been but his jealousy has been so strong that it had blinded him to common sense.

His father felt guilty for he had always pressured the boy to get good results in all his school work although really he knew that Archie was not academic. If only his mother had not died when he was born, perhaps I would have made a better job of bringing the boy up, he thought, but it was too late to worry about that now he had to engage a good Barrister to defend the boy.

Jonathan decided that he would go to Ingrid's house to tell her the news of her proved innocence. When he told her she bust into tears and Jonathan held her until she had calmed herself. Don't cry darling, you can take your exams now that all has been explained. He comforted. No, it's too late to do that Ingrid replied, dabbing her eyes and blowing her nose. I'm too old, and I don't really want to be a solicitor any more, I 'm used to being a legal secretary now and I don't want to go back to being a student. Then why are you crying? Jonathan asked in a puzzled voice. Because I'm so relieved that at last people will believe that I'm innocent Ingrid replied. I believed you Jonathan said. Yes, but you didn't at first did you? She said

That's because I'm a 'not very bright 'male, he said ruefully.

CHAPTER TEN

The next excitement was Beth and Marco's wedding, which was to take place in Italy, for Benito Costa was not strong enough to travel and so the whole family were to go and stay in one of his Hotels. He owned a group of Hotels across Italy as well as some in England. He was negotiating at the moment to join an 'Umbrella 'group for he had only the one child, Marco, and he felt that it would be better for him to be in a group. Benito hoped for a grandson but one could never be sure.

The wedding dress and Bridesmaid's dresses had been made in Milan and according to Belinda, who was one of the Bridesmaid's, the dresses' were wonderful and Beth's Bridal dress was a dream. They all travelled together on a private Jet. Anna said she had never had such a comfortable stress free plane journey before, and the others agreed. At the hotel there were last minute fittings and instructions to be given,. All their official paper work was settled, and although Beth was not a Roman Catholic she had been Christened and Confirmed, and had promised to bring up any children in the faith, so all was in order.

The great day dawned and the weather was perfect, Beth was patted and perfumed her hair set by an expert 'coiffeur' her dress was a fairytale dress in cream silk and lace, and she felt like a princess. Finally they were ready, The Bridesmaid's were sent ahead in a luxurious limousine whilst Beth, and her father, were to follow a little way behind, riding in a Carriage, drawn by white horses decked in plumes and ribbons. Beth would have preferred to ride in a limousine, but she did not want to spoil Benito's pleasure, for he had thought he was pleasing her, when in fact Beth was extremely nervous of horses, to her they always seemed so unpredictable.

The limousine travelled quickly ahead and was soon out of sight. While the carriage and horses trotted sedately far behind. Beth looked anxiously about and her hand stole into her father's comforting hold. Don't be nervous sweetheart, Drew said. Patting her hand, there's nothing to be nervous about we're nearly there. Hardly had the words left his lips when a huge dog came out of nowhere and began to leap about the horses' legs, barking loudly and furiously. The horses immediately began to plunge and whinny in fright and then they bolted. The coachman hauled desperately on the reins shouting and probably, Drew thought, swearing, at the horses.

Drew held Beth protectively to his side and prayed! They had travelled for some distance before the horses panting and sweating finally slowed down, and the coachman jumped from his seat running to the horses' heads apologising profusely in Italian, at least Drew supposed he was apologising. Whatever it was he was saying they were terribly late for the church service and both rather dishevelled. Drew took out his mobile and praying that it would connect with somebody in or near the church he rang Jonathan, who was the Best Man. His phone rang for some time and was finally answered by Seb. What's up Drew? Asked Seb and where are you? Goodness knows where we are, must be several miles away I should think, the blessed horses bolted and we've only just stopped. We're rather wind blown I'm afraid, but still in one piece. Put the coachman on and let Marco speak to him. Seb said. After some conversation the coachman handed back the phone, and Drew spoke again this time to Marco, who told them to stay where they were and a limousine would be sent to collect them. It was not long before the car arrived and they were transported at last to the church. Beth was still trembling from the fright and in tears, until some nuns kindly took her to their Convent nearby, so that she could wash and tidy herself, they even pressed as many ceases out of her gown as possible and mended the tear in her veil Then she was ready to go back to the Church with her father, who had also been able to tidy himself. She paused at the open door of the church and looked down the long Aisle, ahead of her she could see Marco looking back over his shoulder, He smiled, and as the slow measured music of Handel's Largo began, she walk slowly towards Marco and her new life.

After the trauma of the horses and carriage the remainder of the day passed in a dream to Beth, she could not have said afterwards that she remembered anything except her Mother, with tears in her eyes hugging her and giving her a kiss, as she departed for her Honeymoon.

Benito had been very upset because he felt that he had spoiled Beth's Wedding Day, with his idea of a Carriage and horses, but Beth repeatedly assured him that it was not 'spoiled' but just a little unusual.

After the 'First Dance' by the' Newly Weds' it was time to leave for the airport, for although the 'Jet' was a private plane they still had to book a slot on one of the runways. After many 'Good Byes, hugs and kisses' the couple finally managed to leave and drove 'quietly' away, there was no noisy rattle of tin cans tied to the back bumper, for Beth had threatened that anyone who tied old cans to Benito's beautiful Limousine would be in her bad books 'Big Time'

Back in the ballroom the orchestra was playing a slow romantic number and the younger guests drifted on to the dance floor, while the older ones were seated at the small tables around the room, Drinks were served and they settled down for a comfortable chat and exchange of news. Some of the Italian family could speak a little English and so with nods and mimes and odd words here and there they all managed to communicate. It makes me ashamed to say that we English are very lazy when it comes to languages; we always expect the other countries to speak English. Anna remarked as they settled at their table with Angela and Benito. The children at school here have English as a compulsory subject and have to pass all the whole curriculum otherwise they can't go up a grade. Angela replied. This can prove rather awkward if you have a child who wont apply them self or just isn't able to pass the exam, they would stay in a low grade until they do, sometimes you may have a sixteen year old still in a class with eleven year olds. Oh dear, that seems rather harsh Anna said. But I suppose it could act as a spur in some cases.

Jamie Parry seated at their table, was bored with the conversation between his mother and Angela. His gaze wandered around the room. Quite a few couples were dancing now, but he noticed one of the bridesmaids sitting alone at another table. She was a very pretty girl with shiny brown curls and dark eyes. She didn't seem to be with anyone and she sat gazing abstractly at the dancers. Jamie who was usually a shy person felt akin to her, she looked as bored as he felt. He plucked up the courage to go and ask her to dance, 'She can say no, if she doesn't want to' he thought.

Ciara Rossi had notice the handsome young Englishman sitting at the table with her aunt Angela, and wondered who he was, she was surprised and pleased when he came and asked her to dance. She wasn't a very good dancer and, so it proved neither was he. At last laughing they agreed to go and sit down at the table. Jamie accepting two drinks from a passing waiter and seated himself opposite her at the table. Her English was sketchy and Jamie's Italian was nil, but they managed to communicate in spite of this handicap, and Jamie promised himself that he would make an effort to learn Italian now that there was a connections between the two families. The two young people were extremely attracted to each other and although they could not say so in words they were both aware of the attraction. The weekend passed too quickly for the young pair, but at last they reluctantly had to say 'Good bye' or 'Arrivederci' as Jamie had learned. But they had agreed to write to each other in spite of their lack of each other's language.

Jamie struggled with the aid of a dictionary to write to Ciara, often she would not understand his meaning for he did not know the parts of verbs, so that the meaning was lost. Ingrid found him one afternoon when she had come into his office to bring some letters for signing. He was struggling to compose a letter in Italian, and not having much success. Why don't you go to some classes? She asked. I don't really have the time. Jamie replied. We have some urgent cases on at the moment; I just thought I would give this a try for five minutes. I'm afraid I can't help, but I know somebody that would. Ingrid said. Who?" Jamie asked. I'm sure that Marco would help you; he will be pleased to think that you are trying to learn his language. Why don't you ask him?"

Marco when approached was enthusiastic, and Beth said. Why don't you come for dinner once a week and bring Jonathan and Ingrid too, if she doesn't want to do the Italian she can sit and chat with me, although actually I have been trying to learn and with help from Marco, we could all learn together, it would be fun.

The Italian lessons became a regular evening once a week and soon the older family members joined the group, each bringing something, a cake, tart or biscuits to go with the tea and coffee that Beth provided. In a surprisingly short time they all found that they were able to converse in Italian, if only in a limited manner. Next time we go to Italy to visit Marco's family they will be surprised. Beth said. I think that Marco has been a good teacher don't you? She asked proudly and everyone agreed that he had done an excellent job.

CHAPTER ELEVEN

When the Triplets were babies, Janet had employed a nanny to help her with them. Andy was a fully trained nurse and Janet was glad to have him for he was a kind gentle boy and everyone loved him. His friend Isaac was also a nurse and once the Triplets no longer needed Andy, he and Isaac had gone to work in a 'Rest Home' on the outskirts of London. They visited often and were always welcomed by the whole family.

One morning Isaac, out for an early run, looked about him thinking how lovely the summertime woods looked so early in the day. He stopped to stretch his leg muscles and he thought that he heard a fox's scream. Could it be caught in a trap? He listened intently, no it was not an animal, he looked about him there was no sign of anyone only the early morning mist rising from the ground beneath the trees. Then he heard the cry again and was able to move towards the sound, pausing now and then, gradually he pinpointed the sound to a large tree, its roots bulging out of the ground like huge twisted legs. Moving cautiously he neared the tree, but there was nothing there, except a pile of leaves left from the autumn gales and which had not rotted away. This time Isaac moved even closer and as he did so he thought he saw the leaves move.

There was no breeze and Isaac moved closer still. Suddenly out of the leaves a tiny brown arm appeared. Shocked and fearful he carefully cleared the leaves to reveal a bundle of dirty rags, which when unwrapped revealed a baby. The child was newborn, perhaps only a few hours old, for the chord was still attached to her stomach. Feeling for a pulse Isaac thought he could just detect a quiver and so he swiftly unzipped his tracksuit top and gently placed the baby inside it, then, zipping up his jacket and holding the ice- cold little bundle close to him, he hurried as fast as he could back to the Home.

When Isaac arrived holding his precious bundle, Andy

quickly took the baby and bathed her in warm water gently massaging her limbs, he then dabbed her cord with medication and smoothed baby oil onto her tender coffee coloured skin. As he wrapped her into a soft warm blanket the baby opened her eyes and looked at Andy with beautiful dark brown eyes. Reluctantly handing her to Isaac, he said, I wont be long, I'm going to the Chemist. When he returned he carried nappies, toiletries, bottles, formula and six babygrows. Quickly he set about tending the baby with practiced skill, and then he once more laid the baby in Isaac's arms and said sadly, I suppose I should ring the Police now.

It did not take the police long to arrive accompanied by a Welfare Officer. The dirty rag in which the baby had been wrapped was placed in a plastic evidence bag, and Isaac was asked if he would go and show them exactly where he had discovered the baby. Andy asked if they were taking the baby to a Children's Home because he would like to keep in touch and see her sometimes. The Welfare Officer was not sure where there would be a place for her as they were short of Foster Homes at the moment. Andy asked if it would be possible for him to care for the baby for the time being, although he knew that it would not be allowed, for Foster Parents had to be well vetted and it took time. The Officer said she would bear his offer in mind, but Andy felt that she was only saying that to be kind.

During the evening Andy had a call from the Welfare Officer. She had been unable to place the baby for the moment, and had checked Andy and Isaac's records which were held because of their work at the Rest Home, and to their delight, the Welfare Officer was accepting their offer. It's very unusual that we would do this, she explained, but we are desperate. And so the little unwanted baby arrived at her new Home. They called her Tina because she was so small, everyone loved her and she became every one's 'little girl' no baby could ever have been loved more than this one. It was never discovered who had abandoned her and in time Isaac hoped to be able to adopt her.

Andy and Isaac had been friends for years and they looked upon each other as brothers. They had once both been engaged to be married, but it had not worked out. Both of the girls had left, because they wanted them to get more lucrative jobs. Neither of them wanted to go through so much angst again and so had remained single. Now that Isaac had adopted Tina she had filled a gap in their lives and he felt that he would like to have her christened. Eventually it was decided to set a date for the christening, and if the Vicar were agreeable, the service would be held in the 'Lindens Rest Home'. The elderly Residents had not had such excitement since the day when Bruce and Myra their two superintendents had been married there, and they were all eagerly looking forward to the occasion.

The Parry's, and the Harris families and friends had been invited to the occasion and there was much discussion amongst the staff as to how everyone could be seated, but at last all was prepared.

During the Christening service, baby Tina, looked adorable dressed in a beautiful silk gown, she was wakeful and quiet until the last moment, then, as she was handed to Isaac, she stretched out her little arms and much to his delight, she said "Dadda" a gasp of delight came from the congregation, for it was the first word she had ever said.

At the party all the ladies wanted to hold the 'baby' until eventually she became tired and a little fractious and Isaac deemed it was time for her to retire from her admirers and go to bed.

Janet was chatting happily with Anna, when she suddenly stopped and stared, transfixed. Anna alarmed for a moment shook her arm gently. What's the matter Janet? She asked. Janet whispered' It can't be, not after all these years. What is it? urged Anna, by now really anxious. It can't be him. Janet whispered. Who can't it be? Anna asked once more. It's Bruce, my ex-boyfriend. Janet whispered. What! Anna exclaimed. Are you sure? Janet nodded. Yes, but what am I going to do?

Well, calm down for a start, and then go and speak to him, the practical Anna replied. What if he makes a fuss? Said Janet said. Why would he do that? Anna asked

It was years ago and you have both moved on. I must find Seb.Janet replied, rising from her seat. But when she found Seb he was already talking to Bruce and she was just in time to be introduced to his wife Myra. Surprisingly they proved to be an ordinary happily married couple, sadly with no children, and Janet wondered why she had been so silly as to panic. Donny when introduced to Bruce was intrigued. I do vaguely remember you he said, it was when you rescued me from some thugs, I was in some sort of cellar, and 'Boy' was I glad to see you and get out of there. Perhaps I should say 'Thank you' even if it is a little late. And smiling, he shook Bruce's hand. Myra knew the story and also the reason for Bruce and Janet's break up, and she was pleased to meet them all. She did not think that Donny looked anything like the little boy that Bruce had once described to her, but he had grown into a fine handsome young man and she was sure that his parents must feel proud of him.

Janet had always hoped that she would not meet Bruce again, for although she had been grateful to him for rescuing Donny from the kidnappers, it had caused a great deal of stress for her and others that she cared for and she did not want to be reminded of it. After chatting for a while with both Bruce and his wife, she realised that Bruce had grown up at last, into a sensible responsible man, mainly due to his sensible little wife whom he adored as much as she did him, and they all parted on good terms without making any further arrangements to meet. Even a week later they were all still saying what a lovely Celebration it had been and what a coincidence it had been that Bruce worked at that particular Rest Home with Andy and Isaac.

The excitement of the Celebration Day was nothing compared to that of the excitement and delight when a week later they had a visit from Belinda and Donny with the welcome news that Belinda was pregnant.

CHAPTER TWELVE

Janet was even more pleased than the young couple if that were possible. Oh I must get some wool and start knitting. She exclaimed, after she had hugged and kissed both of them. What colour shall I get maybe white would be best, what do you think? Donny laughed. Hold on Mum you've got months to decide that and anyway it's too early to know, you'll have to wait for the scan to find out.

Have you told the rest of the family yet? Janet asked. No, we wanted to tell you and Dad first. Donny replied. Sit down Belinda I'll put the kettle on. Janet said. How have you been keeping so far? Not too bad, just a bit queasy in the mornings but so far I'm OK Belinda replied. Dry toast and a cup of tea before you get out of bed used to work for me advised Janet. So Donny, I shall be checking that you are pampering your wife. Janet laughed. Oh Donny's very good at the moment, but I don't know what he will be like at getting up in the night. He sleeps like a log, a' Marching Band' could tramp through the bedroom and it wouldn't wake him. Belinda said teasingly. Hey stop giving away all my diversionary tactics. Donny protested. The kettles boiling Mum, he said, by way of distraction.

When told the news the whole family were full of delight and congratulations with plenty of offers to 'baby-sit'. What about in the middle of the night? Donny asked.

That's your privilege. Drew laughed. Believe me you can't get out of that one, you wouldn't believe the power of a tiny baby's lungs in the middle of the night.

Would you prefer a girl or a boy? Anna asked. I just want a healthy baby with everything complete. Belinda replied. But I do wish that Mum and Aunty could have lived to see it. She said sadly. I know it wouldn't be the same, but I'm happy to be a surrogate Mum if you want me. Janet said gently. I would love that. Belinda. Replied. I've always thought how lucky Donny is to have you for his mother.

Ciara was to have a big twenty- first birthday party and the 'English' families were all invited. The 'Jet' plane was once again to take them all to Italy. At the airport there seemed to be so much luggage, but eventually all were settled. Luckily Belinda was able to fly as she was past her 'trimester' and not too far advanced in her pregnancy, she would have been very disappointed if she hadn't been able to travel, because she was longing to try out her Italian on someone else besides Marco.

Jamie and Ciara had already decided that they wanted to marry, but Jamie had yet to ask Ciara's Papa. He planned to ask him, and if possible announce it at the party. Jamie knew that Ciara's Papa would have many questions and he had prepared all the answers. He had discussed this with his Grandparents one day and they had suggested that as Ciara had finished at Business College and her English was now excellent she should come and lodge with them. She could work in the office with Ingrid, and if she was agreeable, could take a permanent job with them, for they needed an extra secretary now with five of them in the practice. Armed with this information and Ciara's approval Jamie went in search of Signor Rossi.

Jamie found Papa Rossi and explained the best he could in his limited Italian speech that he wished to marry his eldest daughter. After many questions to which Jamie had the prepared answered, signor Rossi agreed. He had three daughters and although he loved them he could not resist an offer as good as this for his eldest daughter even though it meant that she would live in another country.

The Engagement was announced at the party with congratulations and excitement from everyone. Jamie had bought the ring with him hoping that all would turn out as it had.

All our 'chicks' are leaving the nest. Anna sighed, when the engagement was announced. Yes but they are bringing more 'chicks' back with them and soon you will say that there are too many. Drew replied teasingly. No, I would never say that, there could never too many especially when the babies arrive. Anna smiled.

The next event for 'excitement' was the news that the 'twins' would soon be coming home. Caitlin had written to say that their contract was almost finished and that it would not be long before they were home. This however was not strictly true, for she was planning to go on a yachting cruise with one of her rich friends and it would probably be only Annabelle who returned, although at the moment she too was not sure if she would be home yet, for she was having a 'Romance' dilemma and was not sure whether to stay or go.

Belle had been caught in a deluge downpour of rain and was about to shelter in a shop doorway when a young man had stepped beside her with a large umbrella, saying. Get under here, where are you going? I'm going to 'Dorita's Dinner' and Thank you, Belle replied, ducking under the umbrella. As they entered Dorita's Diner, Doris, the owner, greeted Belle. Bad isn't it? Come in and get dry, what d' you want? She asked. Is it your usual 'Luv'? Yes please Doris. Belle replied. Would you like a hot drink too? She asked, turning to her 'gallant' rescuer. Yes, I'll have a mug of tea and -- He glanced at the menu board. And two toasted Tea Cakes please. That's a very English menu, if I may say so .He remarked. I should think so too, I'm a born and bred 'Cockney' I am. Doris replied proudly. Really? So what are you doing here in New York, apart from dispensing Tea and Teacakes? He asked. I come over when I married me old man, 'e was American, a soldier 'e was, I'm settled now but it took me a long time. E's dead now but I got two kids grown up and married so I'd never go back. Doris replied, placing two mugs of tea and two plates with the teacakes on the table. You want anythin' else? She asked. They both said. No thank you, and Doris retired behind her tea urn, and began wiping her counter with a damp cloth.

I think we should introduce ourselves don't you? I'm Greg Douglas, he said and held out his hand. Belle shook it, it was a firm shake and she felt a tremor as she touched his hand. She withdrew her hand quickly and picked up her mug of tea. She did not know that Greg had felt it too and he looked at her closely to see if she had felt anything. But Belle had gone to the counter with the mugs and was saying as she returned, Thank you for the tea, my turn next time. And then she was gone, scuttling through the rain, which had now become a light drizzle, Greg smiled, typical girl always in a hurry, he thought, and he too left after bidding Doris Goodbye. He remembered later that the girl had not told him her name. Belle remembered too as she hurried through the rain that she had not told him her name. He was really nice, she thought, I hope I see him again.

When she arrived back at the flat she shared with Caitlin, her twin, she found her sister packing her cases. Where are you going? Belle asked her. I shall be going on a cruise soon, with Freddie. Cate replied. I only have ten more days of my contract left and them I'm off, Hurrah! For sun, sea, and anything else that comes my way.

But aren't you going home to see Mum and Dad? Belle asked. Oh I can go and see them later, but this offer might not come again, and I'm not going to miss it. Cate replied. But you hardly know him; you've only just met. Belle protested. I know all I need to know, he's Freddie Danton-Hughes one of The Danton- Hughes and he's great fun to be with. Where did you meet him? Belle demanded, and how old is he? She added. I don't know how old he is, I've never asked him, and I met him while I was on a photo shoot in California. Any more questions 'Mother hen?' Cate replied. I don't think you should go on a trip like that alone with a man you hardly know. Belle said with a frown. Oh don't worry about me; I can take care of myself. Cate boasted. Just because you've had two Judo lessons it wouldn't protect you from a determine man. Belle objected.

Cate laughed. Don't be such a 'worry wart' it'll give you wrinkles. She joked, and Belle gave up in despair. She knew from experience that it was never any use trying to stop Cate when she had made up her mind to a mad scheme, it had always been the same, when they were children, many a scrape the three of them had got into because of Cate and her reckless plans.

Belle worried all night about Cate's trip. And the next day when she was not needed at the Studio, she decided to go and pay Mr, Danton- Hughes a visit. When she arrived at his apartment Block she rang the entry bell and the Porter seeing her and thinking that she was Cate, opened the door.

The elevator deposited her at the door of the Penthouse. Belle took a deep breath and rang the bell. Freddie looking at the screen above the door and thinking it was Cate opened the door saying. Hullo Honey I thought you were tied up till this afternoon, I'm sure glad to see you I'm sick of this paper work, it gives me an excuse for a break. Belle followed him into the lounge, and he offered to take her coat. But Belle shook her head. I'm not stopping Mr.Danton- Hughes. She said. What's the matter Honey, have I done something to upset you? He asked looking puzzled. No Mr Danton-Hughes as far as I know you've done nothing to up set me except for offering to take my sister away on a cruise, don't you think it would have been nice if you had mentioned it to me so that a member of her family would know where she is. Freddie looked at her in amazement. I thought you were Cate, I'm sorry but I didn't know that she had a sister, let alone a double.

We're twins of triplets, and my brother is the third triplet. Gee that's some burden for a brother to bear, two sisters like you and Cate. Freddie exclaimed with a grin. That's as may be, but I still don't think that Cate should be going away with you alone. Oh we won't be on our own, Freddie replied. There's a party of us going. I wouldn't compromise Cate like that, and I would never hurt her, I think too highly of her. She's a 'nice' girl not one of these 'good timers', that's what I love about her. Freddie said seriously.

Belle felt stupid now, but she said. Well I apologise if I

was over protective, but I'm the eldest and have always had to get her out of scrapes, she would lead Jonathan into them too, and if Donny my elder brother was not there I always had to rescue her. Gee your Mom had her hands full with that lot. She must be a Saint. Freddie said admiringly. Yes, she is very 'special' Belle agreed. And she would have been here too if she were in my position. She rose from her chair and turned towards the door. Thank you for your time Mr.Danton-Hughes. I hope you all have a good holiday. Would you like to come too? There's plenty of room and you're welcome. Freddie invited. Thank you, but I shall be going home very soon, they're expecting us, at least they were, but I'll make excuses for Cate and hope she turns up before too long. You'll take good care of her won't you? She's very special to us all. She smiled at him and he thought 'How could I have mistaken her for Cate, she's entirely different in every way except in her appearance.

When Belle arrived back at their apartment, Cate was already there she had showered and was blow-drying her hair. Hi, where have you been I thought you had the afternoon off. She greeted her sister. Yes I did, I had a few errands to run, but I've done now. Belle replied. Are you out tonight then? Yes there's a party of us going to the Theatre, If I had known you were free I could have asked Freddie to get a ticket for you, it may not be too late shall I ask him to try? Cate offered. No Thank you, there are a few things I want to get done, but I hope you have a good time, Do you know what show it is? I don't know, I didn't ask, but I shall be happy to be with Freddie, never mind what we see. Cate replied. You're getting very fond of him, aren't you? Belle said. Yes I'm afraid I am, and I shouldn't be. Cate replied. Why ever not? Belle asked. Because men like him would very rarely want a nobody like me when they have so many 'High Class' girls to choose from. Cate said sadly. Well I think that he would be lucky to have somebody like you who would want him for himself and not his money. Belle replied indignantly.

Unknown to the sisters Freddie was thinking exactly the same thing, and he made up his mind that on the cruise he would ask Cate to marry him.

The next day at lunchtime, Cate offered to get the 'carryout' coffee for them and hurried along to Dorita's. As she entered a man was coming out. "Hi" he greeted, have you got time to come and drink your coffee with me? Cate gave him an icy stare and hurried into the Diner ignoring him. Greg looked at her retreating back in amazement. 'What had he done to warrant that treatment? 'I felt that she and I had a rapport between us but I must have been mistaken,' he thought. Cate was thinking, 'what a jerk expecting me to go along with that old pick- up line' but she soon forgot about it when her mobile rang and it was Freddie

Belle had often looked out for Greg when she went to Dorita's, but she didn't see him until several days later as she was leaving the Office Building and he was passing. She smiled at him saying pleasantly "Hullo" But he gave her a cold look and passed on. Belle stood for a moment gazing after him puzzled by his behaviour, after their previous friendly conversation in Dorita's. She felt hurt as well as puzzled. If he doesn't want to be friends at least he could be civil. ' I thought he was a nice person' She was disappointed, but pushed the thoughts to one side when she had a phone call from her Mother, to tell her that Belinda was expecting a baby.

She was really looking forward to going home she had missed them all and felt sorry that she had missed all the events that had occurred in the two years since she had been away.

Cate wanted Belle to go on the cruise with her and Freddie had also repeated his offer for her to go with them. Belle hated cruises and politely refused, besides, she had promised her mother that she would go home, and she knew that her mother would be disappointed if she did not go. And so she waved Cate off on her holiday with Freddie and prepared to get herself ready for her own journey.

When Belle came out of the arrivals door in the airport, a sea of smiling faces greeted her, it seemed as if the whole family had come to meet her. Hugs and kisses were exchanged and then she was taken home in style like the returning Prodigal.

CHAPTER THIRTEEN

Once aboard the Yacht, Cate unpacked her bags, and hung up her Clothes. After showing her to her Cabin, Freddie had gone on to his own cabin next door. Before long she heard the throbbing sound of the engines, and then a tap on her door, it was Freddie. Would you like to come up on deck and see our departure? He asked. Yes, I'd love to. Cate replied smiling,

Up on the deck she was introduced to the other guests who had also come to watch. As the boat slowly pulled way from the dock Cate had the strange sensation that it was the land moving away and not them and when she told Freddie, he laughed. Yes I get that feeling too; it's just an illusion. I've brought some 'sea sick' tablets with me; do you think I'll need them? Cate asked. Freddie looked at the grey skies above and grimaced Who can say, but at the moment no storms seems to be predicted, and this is a very sturdy vessel which had weathered many storms, so there's no need to worry just take your pills and enjoy yourself he advised.

Freddie knocked on her door as Cate finished dressing for dinner. He called. Are you ready Honey? Yes, come in, she replied. I'm putting on my earrings, but I'm having a little difficulty with them, they're new. Freddie came closer and lifting her hair away from her face peered at the offending jewellery. Ah I see the trouble, here let me do it for you he offered, Cate handed him the earring and Freddie gently fitted it into position. He was so close that she could feel his warm clean smelling breath against her cheek .She turned to say thank you and Freddie gently kissed her lips, he paused for a moment waiting for a protest and when none came he took her in his arms and really kissed her, then groaning he said. Gee Honey we have to get married I can't be on my best behaviour forever and I could never part with you, so will you? Will I what? Cate asked feeling confused. Will you marry me?

73

Freddie repeated. Please, I know I'm not much of a catch for a lovely girl like you, but I do sincerely love you. Cate looked into his blue- grey eyes and at his kind anxious face and replied. How could I not marry you darling Freddie, when I love you so much? I wish I'd asked you before we came on board then we could have chosen a ring for you. Freddie complained. I have a dress ring that we could use if you like. Cate said. Yes, then we can announce our engagement at dinner tonight. Freddie agreed with enthusiasm.

The announcement was greeted with pleasure by all of the guests, except for one man who had been late coming aboard and Cate had not met him. When she was introduced to him her heart sank, for it was the man that she had snubbed outside Dorita's Diner, and now she felt very uncomfortable.

Greg recognised her immediately. And thought ' no wonder she wasn't interested in me she had a bigger fish to catch, I thought she was a genuinely nice girl but it seems that I was wrong' When they seated themselves at the table he made sure that he was sitting as far away from her as possible.

Freddie insisted on having a' Champagne Toast' to celebrate their engagement and the impromptu party became very 'Jolly' as the evening wore on. Greg slipped away as soon as he could and was glad that nobody noticed. He went up on deck for a while, the sky was a deep navy blue like velvet and like Cates eyes too, he thought, but shied away from that for the girl he had been dreaming of didn't exist she had just been wishful thinking, the sort of girl that he could really fall for.

Each day was filled with sunshine and fun and Cate loved it all. Sometimes they went ashore to see the sights or go to a market where they sold strange clothes and trinkets. She did once think to herself, 'It's just as well Belle didn't come with us she would have hated it' Unknown to Freddie and herself someone else hated it too. Greg was becoming very restless cooped up on the Yacht and wished that he had not agreed to come. At last he could bear it no more and at the next stop they made he would leave. He excused his leaving to Freddie, by saying that he'd had a text to say that he was needed urgently at his office. Freddie assured him that he could deal with it from his office aboard the Yacht, for he had all the needed communication facilities. But Greg claimed that he had to deal with this crisis in person and so reluctantly, Freddie agreed that they would put him off at the next port they came too.

After dinner that night Freddie was telling Cate of Greg's decision to leave. Cate was pleased for Greg's disapproving glances unnerved her. One of the guests mentioned that they had recently been to Las Vegas and how exciting they had found it. "That's it!" exclaimed Freddie to Cate. When Greg goes to the Airport we'll go too and get a plane to Las Vegas. Pack an over night bag Catie girl, we'll have a 'Ball'

When they berthed at the next Port. Freddie insisted that he would hire a taxi to take Greg to the Airport, and in spite of all Greg's protests he went ahead with his plan, and Freddie and Cate went with him. In the taxi, Cate and Greg said little, but Freddie made up for their silence with his enthusiastic chatter. At the airport it was a relief to Cate when Greg shook hands with Freddie and thanked him for his hospitality, then giving her a brief nod he walked away, 'And I hope we never meet again' Cate thought to herself.

When they walked down the steps from the plane at Las Vegas Cate couldn't believe the heat, it was like a sauna and she was glad that she had worn a light dress. Freddie grinned. It sure is hot Honey, never mind, we'll soon be in the cool 'God bless the man who invented 'Air Conditioning 'and taking her small bag he lead her into the cool building.

I booked the Hotel rooms 'on line' Freddie said, all we need is a taxi and were off. On the way to the Hotel Cate couldn't stop gazing at the passing attractions as they drove through the city. The Brash and Lurid colours, fascinated her, it was just as she had always imagined it would be, everywhere people milling about gazing in wonder or hurrying too fro.

They passed several 'Wedding Chapel's'with loud music and flashing lights. Cate looked at Freddie, her eyes shining. Oh it's wonderful! She exclaimed. Freddie stopped the cab. "Wait for us." He told the man, and taking Cate's arm he drew her from the seat and urged her up the pathway to the door of a Wedding Chapel. Let's get married now, he suggested. What now! Cate exclaimed in amazement. Sure, why not? Freddie replied. Now's as good a time as any, come on Honey please. He begged. But they won't do it at such short notice. Cate protested. Sure they will, they do it all the time, it's their job. Freddie replied. What about a wedding ring and official papers said Cate. We can buy a ring and sort out the papers here. Freddie replied. What about our families? Cate persisted. Oh we can tell them later. Freddie said. Please, please 'Catie Girl', come and be 'mad' together with me he coaxed. Before she knew it she was standing in front of the Celebrant giving and receiving vows for their marriage. When they returned the taxi driver was still sitting patiently outside waiting for them and he drove calmly away without any comment, as if it were the most ordinary occasion that happened every day. Which perhaps it did, Cate thought. Before going back to the Hotel they visited a jewellers and Freddie bought her a beautiful engagement ring and a proper wedding ring for the ring that they had from the Chapel was not gold..

We'll need to get this ring insured Cate cautioned, otherwise I'll be afraid to wear it. They spent a happy weekend going to all the attractions and theatres. Much to her delight Cate won a hundred dollars from a slot machine. I've never been so lucky she declared. No nor have I Honey. Freddie replied hugging her. You're the best thing that ever happened to me.

Back on board the Yacht there were congratulations,

and amazement at their news, nobody looked disapproving, even if they were doubtful of the outcome of such a rapid decision to 'marry in haste' and hopefully not 'repent at leisure.'

The rest of the holiday seemed to fly past and in no time at all they were back in Port, and everyone was saying "Good Bye" and "Thank you" and "How lovely it all had been" and wishing both Freddie and Cate "All the Best." At last they were alone and Freddie dropped into a chair saying Phew! Entertaining is sure exhausting, Honey, I need a rest now.

Back at Freddie's apartment Cate remembered that she had not rung her sister to tell her that she was married. She had to admit to herself that she had been putting off telling her sister for she was sure that Belle would not approve and she didn't want anything to spoil the lovely feeling of 'happiness and rightness' of her marriage to Freddie.

The next morning during breakfast, Freddie asked her. When are you going to call your Folks to tell them we're married? I don't know Cate replied.. Are you regretting it now? He asked. No! 'Never ever' Cate replied positively. It's just that my Family are very big on Family Weddings, you know, everyone there, Granny and Gramps right down to Donny and Belinda's baby, and Andy and Isaac with baby Tina. I haven't even seen her yet, and Belinda's baby is due soon. I don't want to disappoint them all. You can blame me for the Rushed Wedding, I did rush you into it didn't I? Freddie said. But I also wanted to marry you, so it's down to both of us isn't it? Cate replied. What time is it in England now? I don't want to call in the middle of the night. She said. It'll be Three a.m. now in England maybe you'd better wait a while Honey, I don't think this is a good time to ring. Freddie said smiling.

CHAPTER FOURTEEN

When Cate judged it to be Ten a.m. in England she sat on the sofa and began to dial her parents number. Freddie came and sat beside her, putting his arm comfortingly around her, she looked up at him smiling and mouthed 'I love you' Then she heard her mothers voice giving the number and she took a deep breath and said "Hello Mum".

Darling, is that you Cate? Janet exclaimed. Are you all right? She asked anxiously. Belle said you were on holiday and would be coming home later, but she didn't know quite when, are you still in America on land or on board the boat?

Whoa, slow down Mum I can't answer that all at once. Yes I'm ok. No I'm not on the boat and Yes, I'm on land and will be coming home as soon as we get the tickets. Cate replied. Oh, are you bringing a friend with you that will be nice? Janet said. Yes, I'm brining my Best Friend in all the World Mum and I know you will love him too. I hope you will anyway because he's my Husband. Don't be cross Mum it just happened on the spur of the moment, when we were in Las Vegas. Freddie's so lovely I just couldn't refuse him. After a slight pause, Janet said. Well darling if you love him then I'm sure that I will too, hurry up and come home so that we can all get acquainted. After a little more exchanged news they rang off.

Cate looked at Freddie with tears in her eyes. Now you know why I said my Mum was 'Special'. How many mothers would have taken that news and turned it into a complement. Not many that I know, Freddie replied. She didn't even ask if I had money, most I know would have asked that first. I didn't, Cate replied. No, and that was one of the first things I loved about you. You thought I was just a 'drifter' wandering around with no job or prospects and yet when I asked you out you didn't hesitate.

I felt dawn to you straight away, I couldn't help myself you're such a sweet man. Cate said. Is that a good thing to be? Freddie asked. It doesn't sound very 'macho' to me. I don't like 'macho or beefcake' Cate replied, they're usually very vane and not very kind. And you certainly have neither of those faults. I think I'd better book these seats for London or your Mom will think we're not coming Freddie said, giving her a kiss and a hug.

The journey was long and tiring but at last they were landing in London and going out of the arrivals gate. A good portion of the family met them and hugs and kisses all round were exchanged.

Back at the house more relations came and went until both Cate and Freddie felt dazed. Janet felt that it would be a good idea if they both had a nap in the afternoon so that they would be fresh for the evening meal when everyone would be coming.

Wow you sure have a close family. Freddie exclaimed. Don't you like it? Cate asked him.. Yes, I love it; I've never had that kind of rapport with any of my kin. My Dad was always working and my Mom was always doing Charity Functions I don't have any siblings and my Dad expected great things of me. I wasn't a very happy kid I'm afraid. So I got into a lot of trouble at school just to get noticed. Unfortunately it was the wrong notice and I was always getting punishments.

Cate was ashamed to think what a happy carefree and loved childhood she had spent and had not appreciated it until now, so that when she heard what Freddie's childhood had been like, she made up her mind to try and give him a happy marriage similar to that of her parents.

Dinner that evening was a happy gathering, everyone talking at once and asking questions without waiting for answers. Freddie was amazed when he saw Cate and Belle together they were so alike, but he could tell which was which because their attitude was so different. He had never told Cate of Belle's visit to him before they went on the cruise, because he did not want to cause any trouble between the sisters for Cate might have thought that Belle was interfering., but he could understand Belle's concern for her twin. Belle had appreciated his silence and she began to feel that maybe he was not such a 'play boy' after all for in spite of his casual manner he could be serious when necessary.

Freddie's father had an office in London and he had long been urging Freddie to visit there. Freddie had always balked at the idea, but now he began to think differently, for it would be great to be included in such a close affectionate family and he was sure that Cate would prefer it, for she had mentioned that while she had been away she had missed all the important family occasions.

One afternoon he asked Cate if she would mind him going to his father's Office, to see what it was like. You can come too Honey unless you'd rather go round the stores. Freddie told her. I'll come with you to see where it is, and when you go in to talk business, I'll go shopping. There are some birthday gifts I have to get, so I can get them then. Cate replied.

They met up for afternoon tea at Harrods, and as they came out onto the pavement, Freddie said, Hey, I just saw Greg Douglas. I didn't see him Cate said, hoping that he had been mistaken. I'm sure it was Freddie replied. Let's go back in and see. It's gone four o'clock. Cate said. We're going to catch the rush hour if we stop now darling, are you absolutely sure it was him. I'm pretty sure. Freddie replied. But I could be wrong, anyway, you're right we don't want to get caught in the rush, let's go. Cate heaved a sigh of relief and wondered what Greg Douglas was doing in London, and she hoped that he wouldn't stay long.

Belle wanted to change her job for she was tired of jetting about the world on 'fashion shoots' and had decided to find something near home. She had always been interested in Fashion and was knowledgeable about it too. A friend she had made at college had gone into fashion when she left the college. She mentioned to Belle that they were looking for somebody at their Magazine. I don't suppose you'd be interested would you Belle? She asked. What does it involve? Belle asked. When Ella had explained to her she said that she would seriously consider the job. And would let her know soon. She discussed it with her mother when she went home, Janet thought it sounded interesting and might suit Belle, as she was artistic and knowledgeable about Fashion. Belle decided to take the job and rang Ella that evening arranging to go to her office the next day.

The office was in a large office block with other companies in the building. Belle looked carefully at the list beside the lift and saw that the Magazine office was on the fourth floor. She entered the Lift and was about to press the no.4 when another person entered the lift behind her. She turned and received an unpleasant shock. The person entering the lift was the man she had met in Dorita's Diner, who had coldly snubbed her later. Belle quickly turned her back and hoped he had not recognised her. Greg had seen her and had also felt shocked, he also turned his back and they travelled up to the fourth floor together. They both exited the lift on the same floor and went to separate offices. Belle heaved a sigh of relief. Thank goodness he was not working in Ella's office.

Ella was pleased to see her and very soon they were deep in explanations and demonstrations. Eventually Belle decided that she would like to take the Job, and the salary was discussed. Ella asked her secretary to bring some coffee, and they chatted for a while catching up on news and happenings since they had been at College together. Belle asked Ella what other firms were on this floor. Ella named the half dozen who had an office there, but Belle didn't recognise any of them.

Belle noticed that Ella was wearing a wedding ring. I didn't know you were married, she said. Yes, Toby and I have been married for quite a while. Our eldest son Ryan is a teenager now and little Luke is ten. He was a late surprise baby. Bless him. He's still young enough to accept a cuddle, and Ryan will accept a hug now and then. Toby is older than me, but he looks so young and fit you wouldn't know it. I met him when I was still in College, he was so sweet and kind to me when I needed help and the rest is history, so to speak. Toby's an usual name; you don't often hear it now. Belle said. Although my uncle Drew has a brother named Toby. I've never met him, he went to America years ago and nobody's heard from him since. What caused that? Ella said. Some sort of quarrel I'm not sure what it was about, but it must have been very intense to cause such a rift. Belle replied. That's so sad, Ella said. I would hate it if that happened with my two boys. Do you use your maiden name at work? Bell asked Ella. Yes, we keep our two businesses separate, its better tax wise. Shall we go out for lunch to celebrate you coming to work with me? Ella suggested. Yes why not? That would be lovely. Said Belle, gathering her coat and bag together.

Mum, why did uncle Drew's brother go away, and never contact him again? Belle asked Janet. Where did you hear that? Janet said. Ella, the girl who I'm going to work for. Was telling me about her Husband who never contacts his family because of a huge row years ago, she doesn't know why they quarrelled, but it must have been something serious to cause such a rift, and it made me think about Uncle Drew's brother, because he acted in the same way didn't he? Well, Janet replied. Nobody ever seems to have heard why Drew and Toby quarrelled, and once when Dad asked Drew for a reason he was told very bluntly to 'Mind his Own Business'. But that was years ago. Who knows what 's happened to him by now. Do you know, Belle said, Ella's husband is called Toby? Wouldn't it be weird if he were the same Toby? It would certainly be a strange coincidence. Janet replied. I've a good mind to ask Ella about it tomorrow. Belle said. Her mother shook her head. I'm not sure if that's a good idea, you might be starting a very awkward situation, by digging into past feuds. She cautioned.

Belle had been thinking how she could find out about the feud between Toby and Drew, and after discarding several plans; she waited until the next morning when she went into the office. During their coffee break she casually asked Ella if she had ever been to America. Ella shook her head. Once years ago when Toby and I were first married, Toby did think of it, but then I had this offer of a really good job in Edinburgh and Toby said that it was too good an opportunity to turn down, and so we went to Edinburgh instead. We've been really happy there and Toby was able to run his business from there, but now that I 'm well established in the fashion world and I need to go to Paris and Milan several times a year, it seemed sensible to move nearer to London, so that I can travel more direct. By the way, Ella said, I'm waiting for a sample of my new labels to come in the post, so if you see them when your opening the Mail will you give them to me right away? Will do! Belle replied, rising and clearing the desk of mugs. Do you never tidy your desk Ella, you haven't changed since college, and you were always untidy then too. They both laughed, Ah! Happy days, Ella said as she left the room. Belle began to tidy the desk, and as she glanced at some of the mail, she did a double take for one of the letters was addressed to

Mrs.T Parry. Now I've got a dilemma, she thought, do I tell her of my suspicions or not? After some thought Belle decided to play it by ear and see what transpired.

That evening when she arrived home Belle told her mother of the strange coincidence. Janet said that this was what she had feared, when Belle had first told her of her theory. Seb came home while they were still discussing the pros and cons of the matter. What's all this then you both look very serious? Have you burnt the dinner? He joked. But when they had explained their dilemma to him, Seb too became serious. Ah! That's a tricky one, He said. If I were in that situation with a brother I would want to mend the breach after all these years, and perhaps the original argument could be solved. It may be that one side is too proud or stubborn to make the first move. Knowing Drew as I do, I would say that it's Toby who is the stubborn one.

I feel more sorry for their parents than anyone. Janet said. Just imagine how we would feel if it were two of our children. What was the argument about anyway, it must have been important to last so long? When Ella first told me that her husband and his brother were estranged, she said that she didn't know the reason, and Toby didn't want to talk about it. Hm! Seb said thoughtfully. Leave it with me I'll put out a few feelers and see what comes up. Now what's for dinner I'm starving?

Arriving home the next evening, Belle was hoping for some news from her father. She wasn't disappointed, for Seb, as straightforward as ever had came straight to the point with Drew and asked him outright what had been the cause of the rift between him and his brother.

Drew was amazed, how did you know anything about that? He asked. It's common knowledge among the family, but nobody ever knew what was the original cause of the rift. Seb replied. Now it has raised its ugly head in the guise of Belle's boss Ella, whose husbands name is Toby Parry. Good Heavens! It's a small world and no mistake exclaimed Drew. I've practically forgotten what the original row was all about, I know it was extremely intense and a great many accusations were bandied about, and a lot of nasty things were said. In fact it came down as to which one could say the nastiest thing to the other. Toby was always jealous of me, I don't know why, you would have to ask him that. Drew said. Well, Seb replied, it all seems to be a storm in a teacup, and after so many years it's about time Toby grew up. Drew said sadly. Even as a child he never would say 'Sorry' and I guess he hasn't changed..

Seb decided that he would go and visit Drew's parents. He had promised Belle that he would sort it all out and so he would try. He guessed that the Parry's must be upset at the loss of their son for so many years, and would welcome the chance to at least write to him, for they were not getting any younger, and surely Toby would not be so pigheaded as to ignore a letter from his mother. The visit was a great success, for Toby's mother was overjoyed to hear after all these years that her son was safe, and she agreed to write to him at once. The letter once written was given to Seb to take back home, and Belle would take it into the office in the morning.

Belle left the letter addressed to Mr.T.Parry.on Ella's desk, among the morning post, she didn't say any thing, and Ella didn't remark on it either, and so the only thing to do was wait and see what happened. Belle hoped that they had got the right Mr.Parry how awful if their guess was wrong.

Toby was very quiet that evening; Don't you feel well darling. Ella asked him? Yes, I'm just wrestling with my conscience that's all. I don't understand what you mean, is it something to do with the business? No it's something that happened before I met you, when I was young and stupid, and I can see now that I was making a lot of suppositions that were wrong, and instead of going and sorting it out I childishly ran away. He took a letter from his jacket and handed it to Ella. This explains most of it, and I'm almost too ashamed to tell you my part.

Ella read the letter from Toby's mother, and for a moment she couldn't speak, her eyes were full of tears and her heart full of sympathy for the mother and anger at the son. Imagine how we would feel if that were our two boys. She cried.. You must write back at once and tell them how sorry and how wrong you were. Imagine going through all that from you, what must she have felt when you disappeared without a word Then Drew had that dreadful accident and could have died, and was then told he would be a cripple for life, in a wheel chair. She must have been distraught poor woman. She did not know where you were or what had happened to you, whether you were even alive. How could you do that to your mother, it was a mean, selfish and childish way to behave. Write to your Mother at once and beg her to forgive you, ask her if you can come and see her and your father to say how sorry you are. You have a great deal of apologising to do to make up to them for all the years they've lost. I'm ashamed of your behaviour towards your parents and I'm just glad that nothing has happened to either of them; imagine how you would have felt then? If you were my son I don't think I could easily forgive you.

Ella went into work the next morning, and when she saw Belle, she said, It was you, wasn't it? What was me? Belle said. You said that your uncle Drew had a brother named Toby, who had left home without trace, and you guessed it could be my Toby. Yes, it did cross my mind, and when I told my Dad about it, he said leave it with him and he would sort it out. No wonder he's such a good solicitor, he always seems to know how to put things right. I didn't mean to interfere; I hope I haven't upset you both. Belle said. No you did the right thing; I would have done the same in your place. Ella replied.

I can imagine just how joyful Toby's mother will be to see him again after so long. Ella replied.

The meeting with Toby's parents was full of joy and tears, explanations and apologies, until at last everyone was almost exhausted with the excitement and emotion. Toby felt awkward at the meeting with Drew, when he remembered all the dreadful jealous things he had shouted at his brother and the suppositions that had now been proved untrue.

Eventually all was forgiven, even if it was harder to forget. It was arranged that Toby would take his parents to meet his family, later they would have a family 'Get Together' to meet all the new members that had arrived over the years when they had been apart.

CHAPTER FIFTEEN

On Monday morning Belle arrived at the Magazine Office promptly at Nine o'clock, she was a little nervous that she might meet 'that man' but thankfully she did not see him. For several days she saw nothing of him. Except for one time when she had gone out to lunch with Melissa, one of the girls at the office, he was coming back, and she had been able to ignore him.

For several weeks this situation continued until Belle thought how ridiculous it had become. Two grown up, and hopefully sensible people, acting so childishly, and so the next time she saw him she deliberately approached him and said, May I speak to you please? . Greg taken by surprise nodded briefly. What did you want? He asked. Could we go somewhere more convenient than this corridor? Belle asked him. He nodded and indicated his office. Opening the door, he followed her in, pulling forward a chair for her; he then sat behind his desk. Belle took a deep breath and began. When we first met in the rainstorm you were very pleasant to me and came into Dorita's Diner with me. But the next time I saw you I said "Hello" and you snubbed me. Why? Greg looked at her and frowned. The second time I met you it was you who snubbed me. He accused. I was coming out of the Diner as you were going in, and I asked if you had time to have coffee with me and you snubbed me and so the next time I met you I'm afraid I very childishly snubbed you. Then on the cruise you gave me dagger looks as if I had no business to be there. He added. What cruise? Belle asked looking puzzled. I've never been on a cruise, I can't think of anything I would dislike more. Greg frowned again, are you telling me that you didn't go on a cruise with Freddie Danton-Hughes. No I did not! But my sister did. Belle replied. Your sister! Greg exclaimed. Yes my 'TWIN sister Belle emphasised. I have an identical twin sister, we're part of triplets, my brother Jonathan is the third triplet but he doesn't look like us he looks like our father and we look like our mother. Belle explained. You saw my twin Caitlin on the cruise, and I am the one in the Diner called Annabelle, commonly known as Cate and Belle.

Oh I'm so sorry, what a mix up, I can't apologise enough, will you ever forgive me for being so crass as to take it out on you? It wasn't you're fault Belle said. It was just a misunderstanding and I'm glad I plucked up the courage at last to speak to you. He nodded. It just shows how stupid we men are, no wonder there are wars because we don't discuss things before we jump to conclusions. Greg replied. Would you come out with me for dinner tonight? Then I can apologise properly. Yes, that would be nice. What time shall we meet? Belle asked him. If you'll give me your address I'll pick you up about 8 o'clock. Greg replied, and if it's raining I'll bring an umbrella he said with a laugh.

Belle was in a flutter, what should she wear? She wanted to look nice, but not too dressed up. At last she settled on a deep blue fitted dress, with a Vee neckline .She hoped that she did not look too daring but she hadn't time to change again, Greg would be here soon and she didn't want him to have to wait while she changed for a third time. When she opened the door to Greg she invited him in to be introduced to her parents. She had told them of the mix up and misunderstanding. They had sympathised with him and told him that he was not the first nor would he probably be the last person to be confused by the close similarity of the girls. But when you know them its easy to tell which is which for they have such different personalities. Greg presented her with a corsage of pink miniature roses to pin on her dress, and then taking her wrap from her he placed it around her shoulders with practiced ease. They both enjoyed the evening and hardly paused for breath. Her expressive little face and deep blue eyes, which matched her dress, fascinated Greg and he thought to himself. 'This is the girl I fell in love with at the Diner I thought I'd never find her again' Belle was thinking on similar lines and she realised how much being at loggerheads with Greg had upset her. Soon they were meeting at lunchtime and again in the evenings and were becoming more and more in love with each other. Cate had accepted the explanation of the mix up and now got along very well with him.

When Belle had first introduced, Greg to her parents they had liked him, and now that they had got to know him well, they realised how right he was for Belle. But they waited for the young couple to discover this for themselves.. Eventually Greg felt he had to tell Belle how he felt, he wasn't sure if Belle felt as he did. They often kissed and hugged but he never took liberties and she didn't invite them.

At last Greg could wait no longer, and so when he brought her home after an evening at the Theatre he drew the car to a stop outside the house and turning to her he said. Belle darling, I'm in love with you, would you marry me, please? The proposal was so unexpected that Belle hesitated and Greg rushed in, I'll understand if you say " No", but I hope you wont. Belle laid her fingers gently across his lips and said, Yes Greg I would love to marry you. Greg gave a sigh of relief then he folded her in his arms and kissed her so that for a while there was no conversation, until Belle said reluctantly, I have to go in now although I wish I could stay, I think I saw the curtain 'twitch 'Mum wont go to bed till I'm safely home. Would you like to come in and join me while I tell her our news? Yes, if it's not too late, I'd like to come in with you. Greg replied.

Janet and Seb had been expecting the news of the engagement, for how could two people so much in love hide it even if they wanted to.

Another wedding the delighted Janet said, but she was sad too that they had not been at Cate and Freddie's wedding. If Cate and Freddie were agreeable perhaps they could have a 'Church Blessing', Seb suggested. It's what they do in Italy, don't you remember when Beth and

Marco were married they went to the Town Hall and had the Civil wedding and then they had the Church Wedding another day. Why don't you suggest it to Cate she might like the idea?" Cate and Freddie when asked were both keen on the suggestion and Cate discussed it with Belle, who thought it a lovely way of making up to their mother for not being at the 'Vegas' Ceremony..

Belinda had been busy all day, cooking to stock up the freezer. She had also been washing and had ironed everything, she was pleased with herself, for she was getting near to her delivery date, 'only two more days' she thought as she settled down with a cup of tea. She went to bed early, for she was tired and her back ached, Donny rubbed her back gently to help ease the tension and they settled down to sleep. But before long, she felt a strong stomach pain, which she tried to ignore, but this was a serious pain not just a slight twinge. And then as she began to get out of bed her waters broke. Donny was already alert and was out of bed in a trice gathering together Belinda's bag which had been prepared for this occasion. Arriving at the hospital Donny grabbed a wheel chair from the line of chairs, settled Belinda into it and followed the nurse who had come to take charge.

It was a long night for both of them, for Belinda it seemed to go on forever and Donny felt so helpless although he did all he could to help her. At last at seven o'clock in the morning their 'seven pound' baby daughter arrived screaming and red faced, but soon calming down when clean and warm she was placed in her delighted father's arms. With some whispered words of affection to Belinda, Donny handed the baby to her, and then telephoned all the parents and grandparents.

News of the baby's arrival ran around the family like 'wild fire' and soon flowers and cards were arriving from everyone until at last Belinda asked Donny to take some of them home for there was no more room on her locker. Soon it was time to go home, Belinda was looking forward to that but was also a little apprehensive for she had never had much dealings with babies and was not sure if she would cope.

She did however cope surprisingly well and luckily the baby settled down very contentedly. They still had not chosen a name for her and so she remained as 'Baby' for a few more days. If we don't choose soon, Donny said, She will grow up to think it's her name. Marco unknowingly solved the problem for he adored the baby, and looked forward to the day when he and Beth would have their own. He always picked the baby up saying, Come Cara to your 'Zio' Marco". And so the baby became 'Cara' and it suited her for she had a sweet little face and a very placid nature.

The excitement of the baby's arrival was soon followed by her Christening and then the two weddings of the twins, Janet began to feel as if all her children were slipping away from her, she knew that she was being silly for they were still as loving as always but they didn't belong to her anymore and she missed that, and soon Jonathan and Ingrid were to be married, he would be her last 'chick' to leave the nest.

CHAPTER SIXTEEN

Here's the Post. Drew said, one morning as, he laid the letters on the table; it looks as if you have one from Scotland. Anna picked up the letter. It's from Robbie, she said, as she slit open the envelope and began to read. Almost at once she cried, Oh! No! What's the matter Drew asked in concern? It's from Robbie to tell us that Mr.Arnold has died. Good Grief, when was this? Drew exclaimed. Anna looked at the letter, Three days ago. The Funeral is next week. I must go Drew; Poor Mrs Arnold must be shattered. Robbie says it was not expected, he wasn't even ill, but he died in his sleep, it was his heart. But nobody knew that he had a bad heart. Well I suppose it's a blessing that he did not suffer, but a terrible shock for his family and friends.

We'll both go, Drew said. I'll ring Robbie now, Anna said picking up the phone. Robbie answered the call and explained what had happened, and gave her the time and place of the Funeral.

The day was bright and sunny, and the Memorial service and burial were very touching, especially the 'Obituary' written by friends, for Robert Arnold had been a well-loved member of the Village, always kind and ready to help anyone, and his loss would be felt by all.

Alistair the eldest grandchild was at University, taking a History Degree, he planned to follow his grandfather as a Historian and perhaps also a writer as his grandfather had been. Heather, his sister was planning to go into Medical Research like Robbie. But Craig the youngest who was only fifteen was unfortunately not academic and so he felt that he was the odd man out, a square peg in a round hole and he didn't fit anywhere into such an academic family. And so child like he became difficult, feeling that it was no use him trying at his school work and so he played about in class or went up on the brae instead of going to school. Robbie and Triona his parents, were beginning to reach the end of their tether with anxiety, for what would Craig do if he did not get an education.

Anna felt very concerned about Hannah Arnold after the Funeral, for she seemed to be in a daze as if she could not believe that Robert had actually gone. She would sit staring absently at nothing, hardly aware that anyone had spoken to her. She was grieving deeply. When they were alone, Anna talked this over with Drew. And they decided that they would invite Hannah to come and stay with them for a little while. Anna remembered how kind and caring Hannah had been when she first came to Scotland to work for Robert. Anna thought she had lost Drew through a stupid misunderstanding and that he might die from a serious Accident. Hannah had been like a second mother to Anna at the time when she needed it most. Now she felt that she had the chance to repay that kindness.

Drew had been spending a lot of time with Craig and felt sure that with patience he could help him. And so he suggested to Anna that perhaps they could invite Craig to come too. We could make the excuse that his Granny would feel less lost amongst strangers if he were there with her. When they explained their plan to Robbie and Triona, they were grateful and agreed that it would help Hannah to get used to being without her 'Soul mate', to be among friends who loved her and in a complete change of scene for a while. Hannah said that she could not bear to be in the big house alone, for the rooms seemed empty and soul- less. You'll feel better when you've had a little holiday, Robbie told her. But Hannah did not agree. I don't want to be alone she said adamantly. When she had gone up to bed, Drew said to Robbie and Triona. Supposing you all moved in here to the big house. Perhaps Hannah could move into your smaller house. Maybe she would not feel so lost in a smaller house. When this plan was put to Hannah, she replied. But I would still be alone wouldn't I?

After more discussions it was agreed that while Hannah was away in London, Robbie and the family would move into the big house and the small house would be let on a short lease, in case the plan did not work or one of the older children were married and needed a home.

And so it was arranged. And they all set out for London.

Once settled in with Anna and Drew, the question of Craig's schooling had to be addressed. After much discussion it was decided that for the moment he should be Home Schooled. Craig had been close to his Grandfather Robert. Alfred also a grandfather had quickly formed a bond with Craig and he offered to help. He had the time and the patience, and Rosemary who had been a schoolteacher before her first marriage, said that although she might not be up to date with all the modern methods, she did not think that teaching a child with kindness and patience had altered very much since her day.

Anna had contacted her friend Petra who was a trained councillor and specialised in depression from loss and child traumas. She had been a great help to Janet when Donny was a child, and had first of all fallen down a Mineshaft pipe and later had been kidnapped by crooks. She had helped him greatly with his trauma and nightmares and she was sure that she could help Hannah and Craig. At first Craig had been resentful and wary, but very soon after he had come to know Petra he began to feel that she was the only one who understood how he felt, and now that he did not have to compete with the other children at school, and be labelled a dunce or a trouble maker, he began to settle down and enjoy his lessons. He had become very fond of Buddy, Rosamond's little dog, and they could often be seen in the park together chasing a ball. One afternoon while they were playing, Craig tripped and hurt his ankle, it was too painful to walk and he was afraid he might have broken something. Buddy ran off, and although Craig called after him repeatedly, he didn't stop but ran as fast as his short legs could carry him. It was getting late and Craig was struggling to walk or rather hop to get back to Alfred and Rosamond's house, when he saw Buddy trotting back to him accompanied by Alfred. Never had Craig been so glad to see anyone as at that moment. I thought I would have to hop all the way home, I'm so pleased to see you he greeted Alfred. You can thank Buddy that you wont have to, Replied Alfred, He was most insistent that I follow him, so I guessed something was wrong .Now put your arm around my shoulder and we'll soon have you home. When they at last returned to the house Rosamond was waiting anxiously. After examining his foot she pronounced that she thought it only a bad sprain, but if it didn't clear up soon they would go to the hospital for a check. All proved satisfactory and Buddy was praised for his part in the rescue.

Rosemary soon realised that Craig's talents lie in his hands not in book learning. One day when he had finished his lessons for the day he had wandered down the garden, drawn by the sound of drilling in the large shed. Inside to his surprise he found Alfred working at a bench with a large piece of wood. Drawing near he asked. What are you doing Gramps? I'm making a stool for one of the little ones birthday, Alfred replied. Craig was fascinated; nobody at home ever did anything as interesting as this. Soon he was Alfred's constant companion, and as soon as he had finished his bookwork he would be in the shed with Alfred learning to smooth down rough wood and varnishing legs until eventually there was a completed stool which only needed to have the Sisal String woven over the top. Alfred soon showed Craig how to weave the string thus making the stool complete.

Alfred realised that Craig had at last found his 'Niche'. and was determined that he would help the boy to fulfil his potential.. During their woodworking times in the shed Alfred had gradually manage to get Craig to open up and tell him of his feelings about his position in the family at home. Craig's sessions with Petra had been a great help and he was beginning to realise that a lot of it had been his own fault not always everyone else's. Although he still could not be an academic like his brother and sister, he realised now that he had other talents and was determined to work on them, even if it meant some bookwork too. He started by making a stool, and progressed to a small coffee table for his mother. Alfred was impressed with his work for a beginner and praised him profusely. Craig felt proud and there and then decided that he would design and make the most beautiful furniture ever seen, and one day he would be famous.

Hannah was beginning to feel a little better and more able to cope with her grief. It would always be there but it was not taking over her life as it had at first. Drew had found a college, which taught trades, and one of them was furniture and Cabinet making. Craig had been enrolled and had settled down there. His instructor said that he had real talent and had high hopes for him. When he was eighteen he promised that he would recommend Craig as an apprentice to a prestigious Company who made 'Custom Made' furniture. But Craig would have to stay in London. This could have proved a problem, but Anna suggested that if his parents agreed he could stay with them in London during term time and go home for the holidays. And so to Anna's delight, for the moment, she had another 'Chick' in her nest.

CHAPTER SEVENTEEN

Little Nina, the abandoned baby whom Isaac had adopted had grown into a lovely girl. When she was small she had always been bandaging her Dolls and her Teddy, playing at Hospitals. She loved to help Andy when he was giving out the medicines to those residents who needed regular medication. Isaac and Andy had always thought that she would want to be a nurse when she grew up. But to their surprise, Tina had a higher aim than that for she told them when she was eighteen that her dream was to be a Doctor. They were thrilled and assured her that if that were her wish they would jointly pay her expenses for University. And so, they proudly sent her off to Medical School.

When the time came and she graduated with Honours they were both so proud that they were speechless with tears of pride. Isaac blessed the day when he had found the tiny little baby, almost as small as a doll, and had brought her home with him. She had created so much love for so many people all her life, and now she declared that she was going to give back all the love in return by helping people get well again.

Tina was doing well at the Hospital where she was well liked and respected for her work. All seemed happy and content. Until one day Tina came home saying that she wanted to have a 'serious talk' with Isaac and Andy.

The 'serious' talk turned out to be more like a huge 'shock'. Tina announced that she had signed up to go to Africa to help in remote Villages where there was no medical help available. Both Isaac and Andy knew that it would be no use trying to dissuade her. But they were deeply fearful for her well being in a strange war torn country so far away from civilisation.

They were anxious that she had all the required injections and fitted her out with a medicine chest of such large proportions, that Tina said she felt it was almost as if she was carrying her own Dispensary with her.

When the dreaded day of parting came there were many tears and Blessings poured on her from the Residents at Linden House, and especially from Isaac and Andy. They both took her to the Airport, hanging on to the last moments together. There they met up with some of the other young people who were going. There were three doctors; including Tina, a man and an older woman who was a surgeon. Finally with one last kiss and hug and a reminder to let them know when she had arrived safely, for they had bought her a state of the art phone, although goodness knows if there would be any where to re-charge it. Then one last hug and she was gone. Andy drove home in silence. Isaac sat beside him in silent misery, and Andy who had no words to comfort him, thought it best to remain silent too.

Two days later there was an e-mail from Tina to tell them that they had all arrived safely and were all kitted out for their journey to the first Village, and it was unlikely that she would be able to send them any more messages until they returned to base, and she did not know when that would be.

Tina and the nurses were excited and nervous about the trip into the unknown. It had all sounded so noble and selfless when they had first decided to come out here. But the reality was not so romantic, for the heat in the day was unbearable and at night it was still horribly humid, and the insects were just as much nuisance at night, as they were in the day. Before they left their hammocks in the morning they had to make sure that there were no snakes or spiders in their shoes or clothing .One girl had found a snake and had made such a fuss that she was reprimanded severely by the Lady Surgeon who was in charge of the party.

On the first day they crowded into an old lorry, driven by a young black man, He spoke a few words of English, but luckily the Lady Surgeon whose name was Ursula, and Daniel the other doctor could speak his native language and so they managed to set off on their journey to the first Village without too much delay.

At first Tina looked about her with interest, but the track was so primitive and the lorry jolted so severely that after several hours, It stopped being interesting and became exhausting, and all the girls were glad when they finally arrived and they were able to get out of the lorry and stand on firm round. With the help of the lorry driver they all managed to set up the camp and 'Hospital Tent'. It seemed that the Lorry driver was to be a Jack-of-all-trades, for he was called upon to give a helping hand with everything. He did not seem to mind and would smile and nod when asked to do something by one of the girls.

Tomorrow would be the first day when the 'Hospital' was open Tina had not noticed but during the night a large crowd of people had silently gathered around their camp. They squatted on the ground waiting patiently for attention. Mothers Babies and Children, Frail Old people, and finally Men. There were many simple injuries, which had to be swabbed and dressed but there were some cuts too that had to be stitched.

Tina, going to check that there were no more patients to be tended, noticed a pair of small legs protruding from beneath a bush. They were very small thin legs, and Tina guessed it was a child. She bent down and pushed aside the low branches and received a huge shock. A small child lay there, Tina did not know if it was a boy or a girl for it was covered in blood. Over her shoulder she called, Will somebody help me please? Instantly Daniel the male doctor appeared by her side. What's this? He asked, but before Tina could reply he had seen for himself. He knelt down beside the child feeling for a pulse, and taking swabs from his bag he gently began to wipe the little face free of blood. Then carefully lifting the little mite he motioned with his head for Tina to precede him. Swiftly Tina hurried to the Hospital Tent, and placed a clean sheet of paper on the operating trolley. Tell Bantu I want him, Daniel said, Tina was already halfway out of the tent before he spoke. When Bantu came he took one look at the little boy and shook his head, he spoke to Daniel in his own language, and then he frowned. This is the work of Rebels, Daniel said. This child has escaped from his village to warn the other villagers to flee, but some of them remained to fight. We can't send these people back to their village, Tina said with a worried frown. No we'll direct them towards the settlement. The Militia have guns and will protect them. When we have finished with this lot of patients we'll direct them there too. This lad I'm afraid may not survive he has lost so much blood, but we'll do our best. Tina made up her mind that if she had anything to do with it this little lad would live.

Once all the patients had been treated, they packed up the Hospital tent and packing everything into the lorry, plus a few urgent cases and also the wounded child, they set off for the large and hopefully safer Settlement where there was the protection of modern weapons. Tina had asked Bantu if he knew the little boy's name, but he said he had not seen him before. He had heard of one village that had been completely destroyed and all inhabitants slaughtered. This sounded as if that could have been where the child had received his horrendous wounds. Because he had no name Tina called the little boy Oliver, for she said, Oliver Twist was an orphan and so was this little mite, and Oliver soon became Ollie. Each time Tina tended him, she prayed for the little boy to survive. She did not tell the others for she thought they would think her odd. But to her joy the little boy began to slowly recover. Well I didn't expect that miracle, Daniel remarked when he examined Ollie one morning and saw how well he was recovering. Tina kept her peace and made a mental note to say an extra prayer of 'thanks'. She didn't expect the others to believe in the power of prayer but she did.

The group of Medics had hoped to tour to other Villages, but the Commander at the Settlement would not allow it, he said he could not be responsible for them if they went further a field when the Rebels were so near. And so much to the disappointment of the entire group they stayed close to the Settlement, but there were plenty of villagers who travelled miles to get help from them.

Little Ollie was recovering so well that he was able to walk about the camp, he always stayed close to wherever Tina was. If she move far away he would follow her like a little shadow, until the other girls began to tease her good naturedly, saying that she had her own little body guard.

She taught him to bath himself and gave him one of her T-Shirts to wear. Although she was a small girl, it was still like a dress on Ollie, but he was extremely proud of himself and would strut about the camp like a little Peacock. With Daniels permission she had fixed up a little bed from an empty box and an old sheet complete with obligatory Mosquito net. And Ollie seemed very happy. His body was badly scarred, but his face was not, and he had a sweet cheeky grin. He was always willing to run errands or do some job if it was not too heavy for him. Patients came and went but Ollie stayed, nobody would have expected otherwise. He was their little Mascot.

The Settlement had a Barricade around it for safety sake. There had been several attempted attacks by the Rebels, the girls were terrified, although they tried not to show it in front of the patients, but the Militia had bigger guns and more ammunition and the Rebels were turned away. After an attack Bantu was often busy digging graves. The Rebels did not remove their dead, but they usually took their wounded with them, probably to fight another day.

The heat was getting worse for the summer was now here, and everyone was getting short tempered. During a difficult operation on a man who had been badly wounded, Daniel had shouted at Tina who was assisting him that afternoon. The heat was intense and the Tent was so stuffy that it was almost impossible to breath. Tina had been on Duty for eight hours, there had been so many injured brought in from a big Rebel attack, and all the Staff and doctors were working at full stretch. Daniel had just stitched up his last patient and turned to tell Tina the man was ready for the ward. She didn't appear to hear him for she gave no response, and so he shouted at her impatiently, and at that moment she crumpled down and collapsed onto the floor. Telling one of the nurses to take the patient to the ward. Daniel knelt beside Tina saying. I'm so sorry Tina----- but he got no further for one look at her told him that she was seriously ill. Lifting her up he laid her on the now vacant operating bed, and he began to examine her, she was burning like fire. He knew that his first task must be to reduce her temperature before it turned to pneumonia. He set to work at once, and called for one of the nurses to come and help. They worked furiously and eventually managed to lower her temperature at last. Tina was unconscious for 24 hours and all that while little Ollie sat by her bed like a sentry on duty, and he would not be moved even to eat. Tina was still very ill, probably from some sort if insect bite.

It took several days to for her to fully recover, and even then she was too weak to get out of bed. I'm so sorry to be a burden on the team she apologised to both doctors. How stupid of me to get bitten like that. It could have been any one of us, Ursula comforted her, I'm just thankful that your getting better, How could I face your family if anything had happened to you. I saw at the Airport how deeply they cared for you; I could see that you were their life. I wish that I had somebody who cared that much for me.

Yes, Tina said, I know now that I should have appreciated how hard it would be for them to let me come to such a dangerous place. It can be a big responsibility to be so special to someone. Then she told them the whole story of how Isaac had found her, and how he had adopted her and all about The Lindens and all the lovely Residents who had always made such a fuss of her. What a lovely story, Ursula said. It would make a good film. But I think that we should arrange for you to go home as soon as possible, you need more expert nursing after a Tropical Disease in case it returns before it is clear from your system. What about Oliver? Tina said. I can't leave him behind he might not survive. Ursula looked doubtful, I'm not sure if you can take him with you. She said. I'll make some enquiries for you.

At that moment Daniel came in to see how she was getting on. And Ursula just had to tell him Tina's story. He was impressed, and Tina said that 's why I can't leave Ollie behind. What will happen to him? The Rebels might get him again without our protection. I'll put out some feelers, Daniel replied; leave it with me, I'll see what I can do. I'm not making any promises, but there are a few things I can try.

CHAPTER EIGHTEEN

It was not long before Tina was fit enough to be sent home. She was getting anxious about Ollie, for Daniel had still not been able to tell her what his plans were. Eventually the day came when she really had to leave. She hugged Ollie and kept saying 'I'll try to send for you Ollie if I possibly can'. But Ollie did not understand her and he looked confused. Tina had not seen Daniel for several days and so she was unable to say goodbye to him, but she hugged Ursula and the nurses, for they would be going back home soon, their time abroad was ended.

All the way back to England Tina was worried about Ollie, was he safe and was he fretting for her? Back in England she was taken to the Topical Diseases ward in Hospital for extensive test, and finally she was allowed home. Isaac and Andy were so afraid that they could have lost her that they treated her as if she were made of porcelain, and would hardly let the wind blow on her. But presently as she grew stronger she began to get back on her feet again and talked about going back to work. But they insisted that she must have a thorough Medical and Blood Test, before she did that.

She had not heard anything from Daniel, but some of the nurses had come to see her while she was in Hospital having Tests. Ursula apparently was still out in Africa. It seems that she did not have any family and that was why she had been so impressed by Isaac an Andy's affectionate Goodbyes at the Airport.

Tina returned to her job at the Hospital, it did not seem so mundane now after the terrors and illness she had suffered in Africa. Maybe it had been a foolish mistake to go, she thought, but at least now I have got it out of my system. If I had not gone I would always have wished that I had been brave enough to go.

One day when Tina arrived home from the Hospital, Isaac said. There is an official looking letter for you Tina.

Tina slit open the envelope and began to read the letter; she was so amazed that she handed the letter to Isaac to read. The letter was from Daniel; he had made some progress on his quest to find a way for Ollie to come to England. Because he was a victim of the terrors in Africa he qualified for a chance to come to England for plastic Surgery, paid for by a famous charity. There was no mention of how long he would be able to stay. But Tina was overjoyed to have come this far.

When Ollie at last arrived in England, all the many large buildings over awed him, and he saw so many cars buses and lorries that he felt quite frightened by them. To him they seemed like great noisy monsters as they rushed too and fro along the roads, but gradually he became used to them and learned how to cross the roads safely. He was taken into the Hospital, and he became even more confused when they began giving him tests and taking measurements of his bones. As soon as Tina heard that Ollie had arrived, she went to the Children's ward to find him. Ollie was overjoyed to see Tina and she hugged him and kissed him to show how happy she was to see him.

Presently the Paediatrician came to see him and Tina was able to have a talk with him and ask some questions that she had been wanting answered for some time. The answers to most of her questions were in the notes that the Doctor brought with him. It seemed that Ollie was about six years old and he was fairly healthy, his scars were extensive but not inoperable. He would have one scar patched at a time and between times he could go to stay with Tina at Linden House, where there were two Nurses and a Doctor to take care of him. There was still no sign of Daniel, but Tina was delighted with the arrangements and would have liked to thank Daniel for his help.

It was several weeks before she did see Daniel, and when she did it was entirely unexpected. She was taking the afternoon teas round in Linden House; Most of the Residents were in the Sitting Room except for a couple of them who were resting in their rooms. Ollie was helping her by carrying the sugar bowl round to those who wanted sugar in their tea.

Tina heard someone enter the room. Ollie's English had improved greatly and he said ' Hello man'. Tina looked up in surprise and was delighted to see that it was Daniel. Without thinking what she was doing, Tina flung her arms around him and hugged him saying. How lovely to see you, would you like a cup of tea? . Daniel stood stiffly. What a very warm welcome he said.

How long have you been home, how long is your leave, and has there been any progress on the request for Ollie to stay? Whoa! Daniel exclaimed, one question at a time. Firstly I'm home for good, the powers that be think that I have been abroad in a tropical country long enough. I have Three weeks leave while my blood is tested to see if I'm carrying any infectious diseases and then I'm free, to return to work. Which Hospital are you working in, Tina asked. The same one as you, Daniel replied smiling. For some reason this news really pleased Tina. What a coincidence, Tina said. Oh it was no coincidence, I applied for the job. Daniel said, and he changed the subject by asking how Ollie was settling down. At the moment he did not want Tina to question too closely his motives for wishing to work in the same Hospital as herself.

What about Ollie? Tina asked. I believe we may have found a way. Daniel said. The solicitor for Human Rights working for the Charity, who are sponsoring Ollie, has great hopes of a solution. So keep your fingers crossed, it all looks very good at the moment.

Tina was overjoyed. Thank you so much, she said, choked with her tears. Hey! Daniel exclaimed, putting his arm around her shoulders. That was supposed to be 'Good News' no tears now, cheer up. Ollie sensing that Tina was upset, and seeing her tears, came and stood close beside her, and frowning at Daniel he said 'Bad Man'. Tina knelt beside Ollie and hugged him. No Darling, Daniel is a good man, he wants to help us. Ollie did not look convinced but he stopped glaring at Daniel and putting his arms around

Tina's neck he kissed her cheek. Tina folded him close in her arms and returned his kiss, feeling such a surge of love for the little boy, she did not know what she would do if he was forced to return to that awful place and certain death. Daniel seeing her emotion and how much she loved the little boy prayed that his mission would be successful.

Andy had told Anna and Drew the glad news that Tina was home safely, and also about Ollie. He told them that Tina was worried about Ollie's schooling. Because his English was still not yet fluent enough he would not be able to go to a normal school. Anna suggested that he should speak to Belinda, she teaches small children with difficulties and she was sure that Belinda would be able to help Ollie, if only to give them some information about his schooling..

Belinda when approached was delighted to help, and suggested that Andy or Isaac should bring Ollie two afternoons a week to her, she was now working part time and would be at home. Ollie proved to be a very fast learner, perhaps because he was anxious to please Tina, or it was just that he wanted to be able to speak to everyone, for he was a very friendly little boy, in fact so friendly that he would have gone off with the Devil himself if they had not kept a strict eye on him. Tina vowed that as soon as Ollie could communicate sufficiently she would warn him of the dangers of being too trusting with strangers.

It did not take Ollie long to speak fluently and with the fact that he had put on some weight, he proved to be a very handsome little boy. The ladies at Linden House teased. Oh, he will break a few hearts when he grows up; our Ollie is such a handsome boy. Tina had replied, I hope he will have a kinder disposition than to do that.

Tina was busy at the Hospital, but she often had time to have lunch with Daniel. His excuse was that he liked to hear how Ollie was progressing, this was true, but he also wanted to be with Tina. He had never been any good at chatting with young girls, for as a young student his aim was to please his immigrant parents by doing well at school and achieving his ambition to be a doctor. Now that he was a Registrar, he felt that he was beginning to achieve his goal. But could he achieve his next ambition, only Tina would be able to tell him that.

One morning Tina received a letter from the authorities telling her that the application for Ollie's residency in Britain had been granted. Tina was so amazed that she couldn't at first take it in. How had this happened she asked? Neither Isaac nor Andy could understand it either, but were both as delighted as Tina. The next day Tina had a phone call from Daniel to ask her if she had received the letter. He explained some of the procedure to her, it seemed very complicated to her, but however it had been settled she was grateful to Daniel for his help and guidance. It was so kind of you to go to all that trouble for us, she told Daniel. I would gladly do anything you asked of me he replied, gallantly. Would you let me take you out to dinner to celebrate, he asked? Yes that would be lovely, Tina said. I'll pick you up at 8.0 o'clock this evening, Daniel replied. I'll look forward to it. I must go now my bleeper is ringing.

Tina was thrilled to be going out with Daniel even if it was only a meal. She had really had a crush on him ever since they were out in Africa. But she thought that he never noticed her. Oh well I expect he's just being polite, or maybe he wants to discuss Ollie's future, she thought as she replaced the telephone receiver.

Ollie was now extremely fluent in his English language so much so it seemed as if he had always lived in England. It was time now to consider sending him to school. He had been taught at home so far and was very quick to learn. Isaac and Tina felt that he needed to mix with other children of his own age. He was with grownups so much, he needed to play and run about with his own age group, now that his skin surgery was completed, and so Ollie went to school.

CHAPTER NINETEEN

At first Ollie thought that he would not like to be away from Tina, Papa Isaac and Andy. But very soon he settled down and made some little friends. He proved to be a very bright happy little boy who had no trouble learning his lessons.

Another new boy came into the class at the same time as Ollie. He was not a bright happy little boy like Ollie, and for some reason, probably jealousy he decided that he did not like Ollie, and made it his sole object to be as obstructive as possible, no matter what Ollie did, Dennis complained about him, saying that he had taken his crayons or broken his pencil. Ollie bore with this for a while and then he began to avoid Dennis as much as possible, but Dennis pursued him and at last Ollie became annoyed. Please stop following me Dennis, he said, you're getting on my nerves. But Dennis didn't answer, and the silent menace continued. At last Ollie could bear it no longer and complained to Tina about it. Have you told your teacher she asked him? No, Ollie replied, I don't want to be a tell tale. but he is really getting on my nerves, I have asked him to stop but he never does and he never says why he is doing it. Tina worried about it for a short while and then she phoned her friend who was a child psychiatrist and asked her advice. Jane said it was difficult to say without speaking to Dennis, But it could be that he wanted to be Ollie's friend but didn't have the courage to say so, or it could be jealousy. Well what should I do? Tina asked, should I speak to the teacher or to the child himself. I think perhaps you should first speak to the teacher, she may have noticed it herself and have some plan in mind. Tina decided to speak to Mrs Jackson the Head Mistress and see what she had to say.

The following day Tina rang the Head Mistress and asked for her advice. Mrs Jackson was very helpful. Ollie's teacher, Miss Mills, had already spoken to her about Dennis and they were keeping an eye on him and his behaviour for the moment. Yes but that doesn't help Ollie does it? Tina said, it is getting so that he doesn't want to go to school now, and he was so happy there before. Perhaps you could explain to him that Dennis doesn't mean any harm, but is struggling to settle down in a strange class, said Mrs Jackson.

That evening when she was putting Ollie to bed he said. Do I have to go to school tomorrow? Why! Do you feel ill darling? Tina asked him. No, but I don't like it any more. Ollie replied. But you love school, and all your friends, Tina replied. Well I don't any more, Ollie said, pulling the duvet up over his head. Tina was concerned; this was becoming a real problem, which had to be addressed before it got out of hand. She sat on the side of the bed and pulled back the covers from Ollie's head. Why don't you want to go to school, she asked him. For a moment Ollie didn't answer, and then he told her. It seemed that Dennis had begun by standing next to Ollie and not saying anything. Then he had progressed to taking Ollie's pencil or crayons, and when Ollie had asked him not to do so Dennis had said nothing only stared at him. Perhaps he can't hear you, Tina suggested. But he can hear, protested Ollie, for once when I asked him to pass me a piece of paper he did. Does he ever speak? Tina asked. Not often, Ollie said. But he can speak if he wants to, although he doesn't say much. Tina was at a loss to know what to think, but she was sure that Ollie must go to school as usual the next day. She comforted him as best she could, tucked him in and kissed him goodnight. Ollie lay in bed thinking, and he made up his mind that tomorrow he would not go to school.

The following morning Ollie was up early and ready for school, he came in to breakfast as usual with his school bag packed and ready. But what Tina did not know was that it was not packed with books but bread and jam sandwiches and a bottle of water, which Ollie had risen extremely early to pack in his bag. He set out for school with Tina, but as soon as Tina had gone, Ollie hurried away in the opposite direction. Where should he go? Running away was all very well but he had not considered where he would run away to. Presently he came to a park and he turned in at the gates. It was a nice day, the sun was shinning and Ollie began to enjoy being free, no school or lessons, and best of all no Dennis following him. He went to the playground and sat on a swing for a while, and then he tried the roundabout, then the slide. When he had been on them all he went on them once again, and then he felt bored. He sat down and ate some of his sandwiches, after that there was nothing else to do that he had not already done. There was nobody in the park to play with or talk to and Ollie began to feel that perhaps this had not been such a good idea, at least even if Dennis did not talk to him, at school there were plenty of other children who did.

He sat on a seat for a while swinging his legs and kicking his heels, then presently, feeling bored he decided that he would go home. But which was the way home? Ollie realised in alarm that he did not know. The sun had gone behind the clouds, and presently it began to rain. Ollie walked as fast as he could, but the way seemed longer than it had this morning and he began to panic, but trudged on wearily, hoping that he was going in the right direction. Presently he met an old man, he had a kind face, and so Ollie asked him if he knew the way to Linden House. The old man looked at him for moment thinking. What is a kid like this doing out alone? And he decided he would find out, perhaps he was running away. The old man told him that he was going in the wrong direction, for Linden House and that it was quite a long way, but he would take him there,. My mane is Tom, What's yours? The man asked. Ollie told him and explained why he was at the park instead of at school, He told him about Dennis and the bullying and how he now hated school. Tom listened sympathetically. Seems to me that you should have told your Ma that if this boy didn't stop then you wouldn't go to school. Going off on your own will give

111

your Ma such a fright and you don't want to upset her do you? Ollie agreed that he didn't and would tell her that he was sorry as soon as he got home. They arrived to an uproar, it had not long been discovered that Ollie had not gone to school that morning; in fact he had not even gone to school at all.

Where have you been? Tina exclaimed. I was just about to call the police. Then she noticed that Ollie was not alone. Who's this then? She asked. This is Tom; I met him when I was coming home, but I was going the wrong way and Tom said that he would bring me home, and he did. Ollie said. I went to a park instead of school; because I just couldn't stand another day of Dennis following me about all the time. Ollie explained. But anything could have happened to you, don't ever do that again Ollie, what would I do if somebody took you away, who knows what might have happened. Tina declared, hugging him then turning to Tom she said, Thank you so much for bringing him home. She could see how weary the old man was and said kindly, Its teatime now would you like to stay with us and have a meal?

After Ollie had been fed, and bathed ready for bed. Tina went in search of Isaac. We shall have to do something about this child who seems to be following Ollie all the time, she said, it must be annoying for him, and will soon affect his lessons if it goes on. Tomorrow I'll go to the school and see if it can be sorted out somehow, it has gone on long enough and Ollie is beginning to hate school. Have you seen this boy? Isaac asked. No, but he seems to be attached to Ollie, or else he doesn't like him and is deliberately trying to annoy him. Tina said. Isaac reminisced, his behaviour is very similar to that of a boy we had at school I remember, he would repeatedly follow one of the boys around for no reason, he left before long and so I don't know what happened to him, but maybe this boy has something wrong with him, it doesn't seem like normal behaviour to me.

After she had put Ollie to bed Tina went into the

residents' sitting room and found Tom sitting there talking to Rosie, one of the ladies. Do you know? , Rosie said indignantly, That Tom has been turned out of his Bed Sitter by a landlord who wants to treble his rent, and he doesn't know what to do. He's 96 years old. It's disgusting to think that a man who fought in the war should come to this just because he's old. Tina was shocked. Where are your belongings Tom? She asked him.? Outside of the building, where I was living. I couldn't carry them they were too heavy Tom replied. Give me the address I'll send somebody to collect them Tina replied. Tina went to find Andy, and after she had told him of Tom's dilemma he agreed that they should take Tom in for the time being until other arrangements had been made for him.

Ollie wanted to know why Tom could not stay with them He's my friend you know? Ollie insisted, and so Tom came to live at the Lindens, he was always a favourite because he had brought Ollie home safely and Tina was more than grateful to him for that.

The next morning Tina went to the school, leaving Ollie at home. She was shown into the headmistress's Office and after greeting her pleasantly, she asked. Have you decided what to do about Dennis, Mrs Jackson? It has come to a pass now with Ollie going off without telling me because he can't stand another day of Dennis and his silent treatment. I don't want to send Ollie to another school because he loves it here but now he is unhappy and yesterday he ran away rather that come here, he used to love school and now he is beginning to hate it, and it's not going to do his education much good one way or another is it? I think that Dennis may have some sort of mental problem and perhaps a different type of school would be better for him. I can recommend a Dr. at the hospital who is qualified in childhood ailments and difficulties. If Dennis' mother agrees I could have a word with the doctor and get an appointment for Dennis.

Mrs Jackson was relieved, she thought that Tina had come for an argument, but instead she offered a solution.

Dennis's mother, when contacted, was at first defensive. She thought that because she was a single mother everyone was picking on her. Mrs Jackson explained the situation between Dennis and Ollie, and she had to admit that she had noticed there was something wrong with Dennis's behaviour, and she agreed to take him to see the doctor. that Tina had advised. Dennis proved to have learning ifficulties and was eventually sent to a Special Needs school, where he settled down and was happy. Ollie went back to school once more, and the grownups all heaved a sigh of relief.

CHAPTER TWENTY

To Daniel, Tina's family seemed to be such a happy close-knit family, that sometimes he felt like an alien. He was an only child and he had always found it difficult to make friends. At school he had wished that he had a brother or sister, at least he would have had someone beside him in the playground. And so he had turned to his books and studied hard so that his parents would be proud of him. Little knowing that he was their 'world'. And they were already more than proud of him. But a child has to be given hugs and kisses and some amount of praise, and Daniels parents were old fashioned in that respect and thought that type of treatment would make him grow up weak and less of a man. The result being that he found it difficult to reveal his feelings, and people often thought him cold and distant.

Isaac and Andy were in the garden at Linden House. They were playing 'tag' with Ollie and Tina. There was a great deal of laughing and giggling from all of them especially from Ollie, who was running away from Isaac, but he was caught, and Isaac swung him up in is arms and hugged and kissed him, and then tipped him into Tina's arms, and she sank down onto the grass with him in her arms pretending that he was too heavy, and they rolled about together on the grass laughing.

Daniel who had arrived unexpectedly, stood watching them all, and a sting of envy mixed with sadness touched him, for it was the sort of childhood he had always longed for, and now it was too late. At that moment Tina saw him standing there, he looked stiff and disapproving. She got up immediately, and lifting Ollie onto his feet, she smiled saying, Hello Daniel come and join the fun, its good exercise.

Daniel demurred, saying that he had only come to see how Ollie was getting on. But I can see that he has settled down, he said. Ollie ran at him and wrapping his arms around Daniels long legs he pushed him, sending them both tumbling down onto the grass, every one laughed except Daniel who felt embarrassed, and struggled to free himself. Tina seeing his embarresment, hurried to help disentangle them, apologising profusely. She put her arm around Ollie saying gently, I think you had better calm down darling, before anyone gets hurt. You should never push anyone Ollie, it is dangerous, supposing Daniel had fallen awkwardly or hit his head against something hard. He could have been badly hurt. I think we are all getting a little over excited. Shall we go in and have a hot drink? She led the way into the house and the others followed. Daniel felt as if he had spoiled all the fun, but nobody seemed to mind and presently he began to feel more comfortable.

Daniel was deeply in love with Tina, she had many male friends but she did not appear to have any one special 'Boy Friend' and she treated them all in the same charming manner. He did not know that Tina was only interested in one man and that was Daniel himself. She sensed that there was more to him than the stiff polite man that was known and respected by everyone. She knew that he lacked confidence in relationships, it could not be his appearance for he was tall and handsome, and his figure athletic. She had never met his family, but guessed from one or two remarks, which he had made, that this was where the problem lay. She puzzled for a time as to how she could help him without seeming to interfere.

At last she put a hypothetical question to a friend who was a child psychiatrist. Jane looked at her for a moment then asked. Is this about somebody that you know? Actually it is, Tina confessed. I'm worried about them and I want to help them if I can. The person is no longer a child, but I thought that if I knew a little about how somebody's childhood affected him when he grew up, I might be able to understand more sympathetically, and also I don't want to make any mistakes with Ollie that might affect him later. You're asking for a' potted' version of the subject, which has taken me years of study to learn, Jane laughed. But I'll do my best.

After her talk with Jane, Tina felt more confident with what she was doing. Apparently she was on the right track with Ollie, and her 'Hypothetical friend' had hang ups from childhood that could take years to reverse. Oh Dear, Tina said, is there anything that would help my friend? There is something that would help. Jane replied smiling. What 's that? Tina asked eagerly. If 'HE' was to fall in love, and I suspect he is already halfway there, and he would benefit greatly from a dose of intense affection from you and Ollie. It's difficult for a shy person to be on the fringe of a close-knit affectionate family group like yours Tina, especially when you've never learned how to be spontaneous with hugs and kisses which is normal in all of your family. Tina thanked Jane and gave her a hug saying. Thank you Jane dear, you're a Star.

After her talk with Jane, Tina thought for some time about what she had been told, and wondered where to begin with her 'Help Daniel' project, for she was determined that she would try to help him to be less stiff and embarrassed when anyone showed him affection.

One afternoon Daniel happened to be visiting when Alfred and Rosamond had also come to visit, Ollie wanted to show them how good he was now at reading, He climbed up onto Alfred's lap and snuggled down comfortably. Alfred hugged him. Which story shall we have then? He asked Ollie. This one is my favourite Ollie said, pointing to the story about a Tiger. Alfred gently brushed Ollie's hair away from his eyes, and kissed the top of his head affectionately. Right then! He said, show me how clever you are. Ollie slowly worked his way through the story. Fortunately it was not a long one, for everyone had heard it many times before. When Ollie had finished he beamed up at Alfred, who hugged him and smiled saying. My word what a clever young man you are! At that moment Tina came in with the tea trolley and Ollie slid from Alfred's lap and hurried to help hand round the tea plates. Alfred said Ollie has been reading to me. How well he is doing after his late start, I'm proud of him. Ollie grinned with pleasure and jumped up and down on the spot and then he began passing round the cake stand.

Daniel watching this little scenario was amazed at how easily and affectionately Alfred had treated Ollie. Tina had once told him that Alfred had been a demon in court many criminals hoping that he would not be the prosecuting council when it was their turn to be judged. And apparently at University he had been a Boxing Champion with a punishing right hook. And yet he had been so gentle, kind and affectionate to a little boy who was not his own family blood, but a little stranger.

Later when Papa Isaac was putting Ollie to bed, and the other guests had gone. Andy and the Carers were settling down the Residents for the evening. Daniel sat in the family sitting room 'Day Dreaming' of the wishes that he doubted would ever come true. He had invited Tina to go to dinner with him and she had gladly accepted for she wanted to continue with her project of helping Daniel with his 'Hang Ups' It was a lovely evening and Tina suggested that as the Restaurant was not very far, perhaps it would be pleasant to walk instead of taking the car, and Daniel agreed.

As they walked Tina casually linked her arm in Daniel's, she had not done this before and wondered if he would object, but he didn't. After a while Tina said. It's so lovely to see how much Ollie loves to be with Alfred, and how kind and affectionate Alfred is towards him. He's such a lovely, gentle, man. But my goodness he can be so fierce and frightening when he's in Court. When I was a teenager I briefly considered going into Law. And so I went and sat in the Public Gallery during one of Alfred's cases. I can tell you I was so glad that I was not the accused, I think I would have confessed, just so that I could be put back into my cell rather than be facing Alfred.

Alfred can be tough and manly when it's needed. But I

don't think that being kind and showing his affection makes him any less of a man do you? Tina asked, smiling up at Daniel. There was no answer for a moment for Daniel was digesting this and realising that Tina meant him to apply this to himself. Then he said, you're perfectly right, I know you are, But I do find it so difficult to be spontaneous. Yes I know you do, Tina replied, but will you try to unbend a little for me? You must know that I would do anything or you Tina, Daniel said. I guess you don't want to hear this, but I have been in love with you ever since we were in Africa together, and when we came back to England. I purposely took the job at the same hospital, but you were always so popular with the boys everywhere you went that I knew you would not be interested in me.

Tina halted in her tracks and flinging her arms around Daniels neck she hugged him saying, I fell in love with you too while I was in Africa and never dreamed that a serious clever Doctor like you would even look at me. Oh I looked all right, Daniel laughed, but I never had the courage to do anything about it. You are going to marry me aren't you, Daniel said anxiously? I would never consider marrying anyone else, Tina replied with a kiss. Come on lets go and celebrate, then go home and tell Papa Isaac and Andy. They will be so pleased. They really like you, and Ollie will be 'over the moon.' Well as long as he doesn't knock me down with his enthusiasm I'll be happy to do that, Daniel replied.

The next longed for wish that came true was the Adoption of Ollie by Tina. One morning an important looking letter had arrived, when it was opened Tina was amazed and delighted to find that it was to confirm her Legal Adoption of Ollie. Daniel's friend at the Charity who had helped them before had been a great help once more, and Ollie was officially registered as hers. Tina felt happier knowing that Ollie was safe and could never be taken away from them.

Daniel did learn with Tina and Ollie's help, to be more

spontaneous with hugs and kisses but was still a little wary of being so towards his parents, although they were not quite so stiff as they had once been.

Tina and Daniel's ' Wedding was a wonderfully happy affair, with so many guests that they had to hire a hall, they enlisted the help of Social Services to transport the residents who were well enough to go to the Celebration, and Daniel had a film taken so that those not well enough to go could see it all too.

Tina was making dinner for the residents of the Home. Cook had gone to her niece's Wedding and Tina had assured her that they would be fine for the day while she was away. There had been a cold lunch as it was summer and now she was preparing the evening meal. Cook had left instructions and all Tina had to do was follow them. Everything was going to plan and Tina was congratulating herself. She gathered the vegetable parings into a bowl and asked Ollie to put them on the compost heap for her. Willingly Ollie took the pan and disappeared down the garden. He was gone for some time. Presently Tina wondered where he was, and went in search of him. She found him crouching over what looked like a black blob of mess. What are you doing Ollie, she asked him. Ollie raised a tear-stained face to her and standing up he pointed to the lump of mess. On closer inspection the lump of mess turned out to be an animal. Tina dropped to her knees beside Ollie, and looked closer. The little animal was covered in blood.. Where had is come from? It was just here like that Ollie explained. Tina went into the shed and picked up a clean rag, she spread it over the animal and gathered it gently together, then carrying it carefully she took it back to the house. Laying her bundle carefully in the sink, Tina unwrapped the cloth and inspected its contents, she ran some warm water and gently bathed the animal, as the mud and blood was washed away the bundle proved to be a puppy, it could not have been born for very long for its eyes were closed but it was still breathing, just!

When it was cleaned she dried it gently. It looked much better but Tina was not sure if it would live. She filled a hot water bottle with hot water and wrapping it in a cloth, put it next to the puppy and covered it with a blanket. I don't know if it will survive she told Ollie but we can only hope. She put the puppy in a box and placed it beside the Aga stove. We can't do more now, only keep an eye on it and pray that it will live.

Tina washed her hands and finished preparing the evening meal. Ollie sat beside the box and watched the puppy. Once the meal was over and all cleared away Tina urged Ollie to get ready for bed. I don't want to leave the puppy, Ollie protested. You can't stay up all night with it, darling, Tina told him we've done all we can. Ollie reluctantly prepared for bed. When Ollie had gone to bed Tina looked at the puppy, It seemed to be moving its head almost as if were seeking something. Tina filled a dropper with milk and put it to the puppy's mouth, it opened its mouth and drank; Tina gave it several more drops of milk until it stopped opening its mouth. She covered it warmly again then left, hoping that she had done the right thing for it.

In the morning when Tina came down to the kitchen she found Ollie there beside the box stroking the puppy and talking to it. Tina gave it some more milk in the dropper, it seemed to be a little livelier this morning, and Ollie and Tina were more hopeful for it. During the day they fed it with milk and it began to look a little better. Ollie sat beside the box all the time. It's a good job this is the summer holidays, and you have time to sit with it. Tina told Ollie.

Ollie sat beside the puppy in the box for three days and there was a big difference. Much to Ollie's joy on the fourth day the puppy raised its head when Ollie was about to give it the milk, and after a week it was trying to struggle up. I think its going to live, Tina said, and Ollie nodded solemnly. I tell you what we'll do we'll take it to the vet this morning. Tina said.

The vet examined the puppy, told them it was a female and in good health in spite of its bad start.

Where did you find it, he asked. When Ollie told him he was amazed at its swift recovery. She's a tough little cookie and no mistake he said. That's what I'll call her Ollie exclaimed. 'Cookie'. But how did she get to be in our garden? Tina said. Obviously somebody didn't want a newborn puppy and so they dumped it over the fence into your garden, was the vet's guess. It's lucky to have fallen in the soft flower bed instead of on the hard path where it would probably have been injured.

Ollie and Tina took the puppy home once more and put her in her box. Can we keep her? Ollie looked so appealing that against her better judgment, Tina said 'Yes'. The vet hadn't been able to say exactly what breed she was and they guessed that was why she had been abandoned.

It wasn't long before Cookie was able to get out of her box and waddle across the floor trying to follow Ollie wherever he went. Now that she was better they were able to see what she realy looked like it was clear that she was of no particular breed, but she had a soft white coat, a sweet little face and small feet, which meant that she would not grow big. Her stumpy tail was always wagging; especially whenever she saw Ollie, and soon she was following him about like a little shadow, for you seldom saw one without the other. She proved to be very popular with the ladies especially; they all loved to stroke and pat her. Altogether, Tina thought, although I never intended to get a dog, it was a good day for all of us when she came.

When she was six weeks old she had her injections and was able to go out to the park. Tina bought her a collar and lead and they took her out, but did not walk far as her legs were little and she was only a baby. But Ollie very proudly held her lead and tried to 'Train 'her to walk not pull and she soon got the hang of it, proving, as Ollie said, that she was a very clever little dog. They never discovered where she came from but she was theirs now and everyone loved her.

CHAPTER TWENTY-ONE

There was new excitement in the Parry household for Beth and Marco were expecting their first baby just before Christmas. And so Janet's knitting needles were 'working overtime' as Seb put it. She never went anywhere without her knitting bag and would sit talking and knitting busily. Anna couldn't knit for she hadn't the patience and so Janet reigned supreme in that department.

There was more excitement and delight when it was discovered that Beth was expecting twins, a boy and a girl. Benito and Angela when told were more than delighted, especially Benito for he had hoped for a grandson, although he would have loved the baby whatever it was. All was going well with her pregnancy and Beth was longing for the last month to pass for it was very tiring carrying two babies. She could now sympathise with her aunt Janet when she had been carrying triplets.

Beth decided that she would put up the new curtains she had bought for the nursery. She set a chair in front of the window, and with the material in one hand she mounted the chair and reached up to attach the first hook, but she could not quite reach the ring for the hook, and leaned further over, before she could stop herself she was falling down and crashed heavily to the floor. She was so shaken that she lay there for a few moments and then tried to get up, but she couldn't. She crawled on her hands and knees into her bedroom and managed to get hold of the phone, ringing Marco at his office, but he was not there. Desperately ringing her mother next, she was relieved to hear her voice. The Ambulance arrived in good time and Beth was soon tucked up in the Maternity ward.

The doctor fought to stop the onset of labour, but it did not work and eventually the two tiny babies were delivered safely. They lay in their incubators like two tiny miniature dolls wearing tiny little hats and with tubes attached to them as if they were plugged in to life, their little hands curled into tiny fists and limbs like transparent sticks. Beth blamed herself for her foolishness in trying to put up the curtains herself instead of waiting for help. Each day she and Marco sat beside the transparent box like cribs and watched them lying motionless, they would not even have known that they were breathing if it had not been for the monitor beside their cots. Each day brought hope for they had survived another night, and that they knew was the most dangerous time, for life was at it's lowest ebb then. Neither of them had ever said so many prayers before.

As the days stretched into weeks everyone began to hope that there would be a happy outcome to this trauma, and when eventually, the babies were at last able to be taken out of their incubators to be held for a few minutes by their parents, there were tears of joy from the Nurses as well as the parents.

Christmas had come and gone, hardly noticed by Beth and Marco, the rest of the family had tried to be enthusiastic but it was difficult, and eventually they gave up, promising themselves that when the babies came home they would have a big party for the Christening.

The Hospital Padre had given the babies a 'Blessing' when they were first born, but Beth wanted a proper Christening. They had been registered as Benjamin, for Benito was a little far out for an English boy, and Alicia because they both liked the name.

When the great day arrived and the two precious little bundles were at last brought home, there were tears of joy as well as smiles from one and all. The babies settled in very quickly, for Beth kept to the routine they had at the hospital. Both she and Marco were tired from night feeds for the babies still had to be fed each hour until they reached the required weight. But neither of them complained for they felt so blessed to have their little ones home and safe.

At the 'Practice' all the partners decided that now Jamie had been there for two years, he should be given his own clients and so they explained to him that they were trusting him with the Family Firm's reputation in giving them to him. Jamie understood this and was keen to do well, for he and Ciara wanted to get married and he realised that he would need a larger income. Accordingly, he began to work on the files given him and to look for a solution to the problems contained there.

The first was a case of shop- lifting. The store manager had stated that an elderly lady had come into the store and blatantly begun to fill her basket with goods to the value of twenty pounds. She had been caught as she went out of the door and the police were called. Jamie read the printed text carefully, twice, and the word that caught his eye was 'elderly'. How 'Elderly' was this lady he wondered. He searched the text again, but there was no mention of her age. Somehow he felt that there should have been. He lifted the phone and asked to speak to one of the lady's family. Her daughter answered him. He explained who he was, and asked, "Would it be possible for you to bring your Mother's Birth Certificate and a recent Medical Report, in for me please?" Mrs Jordan brought the Certificates in that afternoon. Jamie looked at the Age on the Birth Certificate and saw that the 'Elderly' lady was ninety- five years old, and he thought, 'Has this store manager no compassion, to prosecute an old lady for a few paltry groceries'. Is this the very latest health certificate you have for your Mother? He asked Mrs Jorden. Well she hasn't been to the Doctor for some considerable time for she has very good health. She replied. Would you give me your doctor's name and address Jamie asked, or his phone number if you have it with you, I would like to have a word with him if you don't mind. If you would like to sit in the waiting room I will just try to speak to him now. Taking the paper with the phone number that she had given him he opened the door for her to leave.

Doctor Patel was very helpful and agreed with Jamie that this was an unnecessary prosecution that could have been avoided if the manager had used his sense instead of being so officious. The Doctor agreed to go and see the old

126

lady and would phone Jamie with his findings. The next day the Doctor contacted Jamie and said, it's as you suspected. This lady has the beginnings of Alzheimer's and has no clear notion of what she is doing. I will write a report for you and that should clear the matter up. I'm glad you thought to ask me, for I haven't seen her for some time, as her general health is so good. Jamie put the phone down and 'punched the air' One down to me he thought, I must go and tell Dad.

Drew when told of the case was pleased that Jamie had done so well on his first case, but had to warn him that all cases would not be so straight forward, and could sometimes drag on frustratingly.

CHAPTER TWENTY-TWO

It was not long before Jamie and Ciara were planning their wedding, which was to be held in England. It was their choice and secretly the family were glad of that because there were so may of them as well as the babies to transport in would have been very difficult. Ciara's sisters were Bridesmaid's and Marco was to be Best Man. And everyone enjoyed a good time now that the' Family' had learned to speak a little Italian.

Both of the twins were now expecting babies and Jonathan and Ingrid had been hoping for a baby but so far they were disappointed. Belle was sympathetic to her sister-in-law and remembering that her mother had found it difficult to conceive with the triplets she suggested that Ingrid try going to the Holistic Clinic where her mother had gone. I'm not suggesting that you want triplets. Belle laughed, but it is worth a try, you do lead a very busy life with your job as a legal secretary especially working with Jonathan, I'll bet he keeps you on the go, he really should have two secretaries for the amount of work he goes through. Ingrid laughed. Yes for a boy who wasn't sure if he wanted to be a lawyer he certainly took to it with a vengeance.

When Ingrid arrived at the Holistic Clinic it was as Janet had described to her. It didn't seem to have changed very much over the years. It had been re-decorated of course but the methods were the same,

Except that there was no little Beulah to greet her and give her courage. She enjoyed the massage and relaxation classes but found the meditation difficult, she couldn't seem to switch off, her brain kept going round and round like a Hamster in a cage and things that she had left undone to come here kept intruding on her memory. At last she got the hang of it, well almost, she thought, maybe I'm not enough of a believer to benefit, for some of it seemed a little strange, although she went along with it in the hope that it would help her. Jonathan came to meet her and she chatted to him on the way home about the course. Perhaps it's me that need the treatment, he remarked, you never know. They gave me some oil to rub onto myself, before I meditate. Ingrid said, I think we should both use it, what do you think? Can't do any harm Jonathan replied, Might as well get your money's worth. But I'm not sure I can learn to meditate, my brain is so full of work and I can't seem to switch off. They used the oil and then after a while forgot about their problem for a bigger problem arose to occupy them.

Alfred Harris had been in court all day for although he was eighty, his brain was still as sharp as it had ever been. It was a hot day and the court was stuffy. Alfred had felt off colour for a few days but keeping busy had always been his cure for ailments. As he had left the court- room he collapsed, luckily his clerk was there to support him or he could have been injured for he was descending the steps down to the ante- room.

At the hospital he was tested and then settled into bed, although he protested that there was nothing wrong with him. After a few days in hospital he began to recover a little and although one arm was weak he could walk and speak. You were very fortunate Mr Harris, the Doctor said, after Alfred had complained that there was nothing wrong with him now. You could have been much worse, you had a 'Mini Stroke' but you must rest or you could have a 'Full Stroke' next time. Alfred looked stubborn, but Rosamond replied, He is going to rest Doctor, I can guarantee that, for between the family and myself he won't be able to do anything different. Alfred found Buddy a great comfort and enjoyed gentle walks with him in the park each day. Buddy seemed to realise that Alfred could not hurry, and walked sedately beside him, almost as if he were taking care of Alfred,

Alfred grumbled at his forced retirement, but Rosamond reminded him that for years he had said, 'When I retire I shall be able to spend more time doing my woodworking' Why don't you make a project of making a little stool for each of the children and grand children. Rosamond suggested. At the rate the family is growing that should keep you fully occupied for a long time. Alfred said that he would consider the option, but he complained that he was a Barrister not a Carpenter, although to himself he had to admit that it was an idea that appealed to him, for he had always used his DIY as a relaxation, and how hard could it be to make a few little stools? Just to please Rosamond., and so he set about planning and making the stools.

There were quite a few to be done and he thought it would be nice to give them one each for Christmas. Even the babies, for they would soon be old enough to use them. Alfred had been working on the stools for some weeks but had run out of wood, and he went to the wood yard for some more. He took some home with him and ordered the rest to be delivered. On his return he had his arms full and did not notice that he had not closed the side gate properly. In the shed he busily started to tie the stools that he had finished together, and then he collected his carpentry tools ready to use them. Buddy had gone with him to the yard and was now curled up in a box in the corner of the shed.. Alfred had his back to the door, he heard Buddy growl and was about to say What's the matter boy, when he was felled by a mighty blow on his shoulder, and he fell to the ground stunned. Buddy began to bark and the intruder kicked out at him all the while tying the stools into a bundle and putting the expensive tools into a sack. But Buddy was made of sterner stuff than that and a few kicks didn't deter him. He barked and growled with all his might, then leapt at the man and grabbed a large piece if the seat of his jeans. The man yelled but Buddy held him fast. Craig who had been coming down the garden to look for Alfred to tell him that tea was ready, ran to the shed to see what was the matter. He grabbed an old cricket bat used to prop open the door in hot weather and without hesitation he swung it as hard as he could and felled the intruder with a heavy blow. He grabbed some garden twine and twisted it around the intruder's legs before the man came out of his daze, then quickly he dialled 999. The police sirens were whaling and Rosamond came to see what the commotion was about. Alfred was trying to get up and Craig was about to help him to his feet. But the Policeman stopped him, saying that the medics must attend to him first in case of injury. Just then the ambulance men arrived and took over, while the police handcuffed the burglar. Craig picked Buddy up reassuring him and trying to silence him, and at last he managed it, but Buddy still growled in his throat, he was not happy with the situation and wanted to protect his family. While he had been waiting Craig had taken some photos of the crime scene on his phone and the police borrowed the phone for a while. Alfred refused to go to hospital and after various tests the Medics pronounced Alfred able to go into the house, but he was to lie on the sofa or in bed and call his doctor to visit him if he felt at all unwell. . Buddy was praised by everyone for a brave little dog. Craig laughed and said, He may be small but he thinks he is a guard dog to us all. The police were leaving. This one said the officer, indicating the Burglar, is a habitual offender, and this time he will be going down for a long time. Last time he was warned but now he has run his length and will do a long stretch, he's had all his chances.

After a few days rest Alfred felt much better, But Rosamond always made sure the side gate was locked after the frightening incident they had suffered.

Ingrid awoke with a start, looking at the bedside clock she thought 'Help I've overslept' and

Jumping quickly out of bed she grabbed at her dressing gown and as she did so her head swam, she rushed to the bathroom, and was violently sick. Oh no not a tummy bug just what I don't need today, of all days when Jonathan is in court this morning and I haven't finished typing his notes, he didn't give me the revised version till late yesterday. She hurriedly showered and dressed before grabbing some toast and rushing from the house. Jonathan was already at his desk when she arrived at the office. Why didn't you wake me when you got up? She asked. "You looked so peaceful and I thought you needed the rest, we have been rather busy the last couple of days. He replied. I asked Ciara to type out the last of the notes., Everything is in order. Don't worry. He smiled and giving her a hug, he gathered up his papers and files, then departed for court. Ingrid felt much better now and began to file away some reports and sort out what would be needed next day. It must have been something that I ate that didn't agree with me, she thought, and dismissing the brief moment of malaise from her mind she settled down to work.

The trouble was that the 'malaise' as she had thought of it, did not go away, but returned again the next morning. Annoyed with herself, she was especially careful what she ate all the following day, but it made no difference. She rang Beth to ask her what should she get for the twins birthday for they were to be a year old soon, and Ingrid had not had much experience of small children and wanted to be sure to get the right toys. She told Beth of her sickness and Beth laughed. Get a 'Test Kit' she advised. What! Ingrid exclaimed, I'm not pregnant. Are you sure? Beth replied. I've had no signs, Ingrid said. Well it looks as if you've got a sign now, get the ' Kit' Ingrid I think you'll find I'm right.

During her lunch hour Ingrid went and bought a 'Kit' she took it home, reluctant to use it in case she was disappointed. She told Jonathan and he suggested he would wait in the bedroom for her to support her what ever the outcome. Ingrid disappeared into the bathroom and presently she came back handing the 'stick' to Jonathan, one look and he whooped with joy, hugging Ingrid till she was breathless. Janet was sure it was due to the visit to the 'Holistic Clinic.' Jonathan and Ingrid were not sure, although they were happy with the outcome.

When Marcus and Beth married, Benito had bought

132

them a house as a wedding gift. He had done the same for Ciara, his goddaughter, when she married Jamie, and it was just as well, for the small flat where they were living would not have been large enough with the baby they now expected. Papa Rossi was delighted when he heard their news, for he hoped for a grandson, granddaughters were a blessing but a grandson would be a bonus, for who would run the business in the future when he was gone.

Christmas this year was a happy time. Last year nobody felt 'Happy' for the twins were so tiny and weak that nobody knew what would be the outcome. This Year everything was different. The twins had just had their first birthday and were doing well, baby Cara had just taken her first steps, there were five new babies expected, and Alfred was recovering from his stroke. Tina had managed to Adopt Ollie and had married her Daniel. Isaac and Andy were delighted that their family had grown and the news that Tina was now expecting a baby too was the best present they could have had.

Gathered round the Christmas tree at Seb and Janet's house, Seb, handed round the glasses of mulled wine and proposed a toast. Here's to the Family, old, new, and soon to arrive, he said. Turning to Janet and Anna he said, soon your 'Nests' will be full again. A Happy Christmas and a good New Year to all of us. To which sentiment everyone raised a glass, and Buddy gave a Woof! As if in agreement.

THE END

Previous books by Mary Kay.

Sooner or later

Consequences

One Step At A time

.